I0527552

Burnt

A Single Dad, Small Town Romance

By Michael Geraghty

Hold Fast Publishing

Copyright © 2025 by Michael Geraghty & Hold Fast Publishing All rights reserved.

This is a work of fiction. Names, characters, businesses, places, events and incidents are either the products of the author's imagination or used in a fictitious manner. Any resemblance to actual persons, living or dead, or actual events is purely coincidental.

This book contains sexually explicit scenes and adult language.
All characters in this work are 18 years of age or older.

1

Travis

I could hear the fire in the house before I even entered it. My team at Ridgefield Engine Company 32 had set up their perimeter and were working on the outside of the house while Tommy, one of the guys I trusted the most on my team, and I steadily worked our way into the small ranch home on Recker Street that we had gotten the call about just minutes ago. It didn't take long for us to realize that this was a delicate situation. As soon as we entered the front door smoke and heat blasted us. We had both been on the job long enough to know what to do, how to work through everything, and how to move to find if anyone was inside. Neighbors had indicated they thought a mother and daughter were in here somewhere, and we needed to get them out.

I steadied myself through the living room and could see flames were starting to lick the carpeting and the ceiling. We needed to move fast and get to the bedrooms to see about finding anyone and getting them out of here as quick as possible. Tommy and I moved quickly towards the hall. I took the lead, checking doors to make sure they were safe until we got to the back bedroom. Smoke and flames were starting to fill the hallway quickly, and I moved urgently to push the door open and get inside.

There we found the mother, a woman in her thirties, face clearly filled with fright, clutching her daughter. The girl looked up briefly as we came into the room and she looked to be no more than five or six. The woman began shouting in Spanish at us, and neither one of us understood what she was saying. Tommy reached for her and moved her off the bed. I tried to get her to hand me her daughter so we could get out safely, but she kept clutching the girl tighter and tighter. Neither of us understood the other, and I couldn't afford to waste any more time arguing about it. I took the lead and began to work my way back toward the front door.

Tommy, the woman, and the girl were all following closely behind me. Flames were stronger than when we first came in, and they were engulfing the ceiling now, making an exit more treacherous. As I reached the front door, with black smoke now billowing out the door, I turned to Tommy and the woman to pull them towards the exit. Before I could reach them, the ceiling collapsed on top of them as the girl tumbled to the floor in front of me. Instinct took over, and I lifted the girl off the floor before flames could reach her and darted out the door. I quickly passed the girl off to one of my fellow firefighters and turned to go back to help. I had reached the front porch when more of the home collapsed under the weight of flames, water, and smoke, taking me down through the porch up to my waist. I felt my head bang roughly on the wood and knew there was a piece of flooring that had gone right through my suit and into my leg. The combination of the pain, heat, and smoke was overwhelming. My mind raced to Tommy and the woman, to the young girl, and to my own young girl waiting for me at home. I thought about Abby and what would happen to her, and in the haze, I saw her standing there smiling, alongside a familiar face that I had not seen in a long time. I blacked out, struggling against the darkness and the visions.

And then I woke up.

2

Travis

"Dad, I've been calling you for about ten minutes."

Abby looked at me with that frustrated look that any twelve-year-old gets when they think they know more than their parents. I had just peeled my eyes open after having that dream again, the one I had become all too familiar with over the last two months or so since I was injured. I had been placed on disability since the incident, and while the investigation into the fire and the events had cleared me of any wrongdoing, I still felt the weight of heavy guilt over what had happened there. I tried to trudge through each day for Abby's sake, trying to make her last weeks of summer vacation before school started up again a bit better. Of course, she didn't see it that way at all.

"Dad, are you even listening to me?"

I looked up at Abby and saw her standing there, her shoulder-length red hair moving along with the breeze from the air conditioner in my bedroom. She was already dressed in a t-shirt and shorts, ready for another hot August day, and now she was prodding me on to get me moving for something.

"What's up?" I asked her as I wiped my eyes clear and pushed myself up out of bed. The wound in my leg and healed nicely, thankfully, and left me with quite a scar and a bit of a limp after surgery and physical therapy. I hobbled a bit, and Abby braced my right arm and helped me through the door and out into the kitchen.

"I said that guy is on the phone again. The lawyer," she huffed, and she handed me the cordless phone from the kitchen. At this point, I wasn't sure just what lawyer she was talking about since there had been so many of them over the weeks, so I just picked up the phone and started talking.

"Hello," I said gruffly into the phone as I went to pour myself a cup of coffee. Abby quickly reached over and poured it for me instead, so I didn't spill any on the floor or the counter. Thank God for her.

"Mr. Travis Stone?" I heard a squeaky, inquisitive voice on the other end of the phone. He clearly wasn't the lawyer from the union, the disability company or any of the other lawyers I had talked to lately.

"Yes, who is this?" I said, already losing patience with this. I could hear I was on a speakerphone as the person on the other end was rustling paperwork while talking to me.

"Mr. Stone, this is Irv Rogers, I'm a lawyer here in the town of Canon. I've left you a few messages, but I never heard back from you."

Canon was a place I thought I had put behind me a long time ago. Sure, I still had family and friends that lived there, though not nearly as many of either as I had when I left there to go to college. I was pretty sure I knew why this guy was calling now.

"What can I do for you, Mr. Rogers?" A smile crept across my face after I called him Mr. Rogers as I imagined him sitting there in his red sweater and slip-on shoes. I chuckled as I took a sip of my coffee. Abby looked up at me from the kitchen table like I had two heads, shook her head lightly and sighed, and went back to reading her book.

"It's still the matter of your father and his estate Mr. Stone. I really need for you to come out here so we can settle everything."

I sipped some more coffee slowly to clear my head some more. The whole mess of my father passing away had happened just days after the fire, and I had hardly had any time to comprehend it. I had missed the funeral, though I don't know that I would have gone anyway. My father and I hadn't spoken since just after Abby was born, and I didn't really think he had anything anyone could call an estate to leave to someone.

"Isn't this something we can take care of over the phone, or email or fax or something?" I told him as I placed my cup down on the counter. I heard Abby say, "Who uses a fax anymore?" as she giggled at me. I shooed her out of the room with my hands, and she slammed her book closed and headed to her bedroom down the hall. I sat down at the kitchen table, trying to get a handle on what this guy was saying.

"I'm afraid not Mr. Stone," he said to me in a shaky tone. "There are papers and forms to sign for legal purposes. Do you think you can get out here?"

I knew I could get out there; it was more of a question of if I wanted to go. I was on disability, more than likely permanently, and had nothing keeping me here in Ridgefield, which, while a lot bigger, sadly, was not much more exciting than Canon.

"Sure, I can be there tomorrow," I said to him in a resigned tone.

"Oh, fantastic," he replied. I could hear more papers shuffling. "That's wonderful. Just come by my office tomorrow then. I am here by 9. My address is 24 Reese Place. Do you know where that is?"

I only spent the first twenty years of my life there buddy, I thought to myself. I took a deep breath before answering him.

"Yeah, I think I remember where it is," trying not to sound too sarcastic.

"Okay then, I'll see you tomorrow. Have a good day," Mr. Rogers told me as he hung up.

I pressed the off button on the phone and laid it on the table. I stood up, groaning a bit as I heard my knee creak. I looked down at my leg and traced the part of the scar that was visible, going up my right leg from my knee and disappearing under the hem of my sleep shorts as it went further up my thigh. I righted myself and walked down the hall towards Abby's room.

I gently knocked on the door and waited for her to tell me it was okay to enter. This was something I was still getting used to now that she was twelve and demanded a bit more privacy than the days when she begged me to leave her bedroom door open so it wasn't so dark in there. When she didn't respond to my knock after about ten seconds, I slowly opened the door.

Abby was sitting at her desk, her earbuds in as she listened to music on her phone. She was typing away on her laptop as I walked up behind her and placed my left hand on her shoulder.

She spun around, looking at me with shocked eyes, and then slammed her laptop closed.

"Dad!" she shouted at me. "You're supposed to knock before you come in." She pulled out her earbuds, clutched her laptop, and got up and sat cross-legged on her bed.

"You're supposed to respond when I knock," I answered her. Since this wasn't an argument I wanted to get into right now, I decided to just let it go.

"You need to pack some things. We have to go to Canon." I scanned her room, barely recognizing it anymore. Gone were the little girl adornments that she wanted on her walls just a year or so ago. Now her walls had posters and pictures of music bands. Gone were the Disney princesses, replaced by the faces of female singers, actresses, athletes, and writers I barely recognized.

"Why are we going to Canon? Are we going to see Grandma?" Abby's eyes lit up at the prospect of seeing my mother. The two were something of kindred spirits, and my mom was really the only female role model Abby has had in her life since she was born.

"Yes, we'll see Grandma, but I have some other things to take care of there too. We may be there for a bit."

"How long?" Abby asked. She was already getting her suitcases out of her closet and arranging things to pack.

"I'm not really sure," I said to her. "We'll have to see how things go."

"No problem," Abby replied. "There's nothing in this town for me anyway."

"You're too young to sound so jaded," I told her. "I'll go start packing myself."

"Fine," she said to me, walking me to the door. "I'll be ready in ten minutes." Abby closed the door on me as I stood there facing the door. I was going to open the door again, but thought better of it and just headed down to my room to start packing. At least going to Canon was going to be easy for one of us.

3

Sophie

I sat in my classroom, not quite going over the curriculum I was setting up for the new school year set to start in just a week or two. I kept finding my mind wandering, staring out the window to the grassy areas that were freshly mowed by the groundskeeper, and to the places further out and beyond, where you could almost see the back of Stearns's ice cream stand. I heard myself let out an audible sigh, wondering about the world that was outside the school walls, past Stearin's, past the old Howard place where they had a farm for generations, and even beyond Highway 32 and out to the rest of the world.

A light knock on the open classroom door startled me out of my daydreaming. I turned to look and saw Mary Connors, the eighth-grade math teacher in my section of the school, standing there smiling at me. She slowly walked over to my desk and sat herself down on the corner of it.

"What's up Mary?" I asked her as I shut my planner. I knew I wasn't going to get much more accomplished today anyway.

"What's up with me? What's up with you?" she said to me quizzically. "I've been standing there for five minutes watching you stare out the window like you were watching the grass grow. What were you daydreaming about?"

I grabbed my planner and a couple of books from my desk and shoved them into my backpack, the same leather backpack I had managed to hold onto since my college days.

"Oh nothing really," I said to her absentmindedly as I closed the backpack. "Just enjoying the last waning days of summer I guess."

"Sure you were," Mary said sarcastically. Mary and I had started teaching here at Canon Middle School at the same time about eight years ago. Just thinking that it had already been eight years that had gone by was hard to imagine.

"There you go again," Mary said to me as she playfully pushed my shoulder. "We need to do something to snap you out of your doldrums. How about we grab some dinner tonight?"

"I don't know Mary," I told her as we slowly walked down the freshly waxed hallway.

"Come on Sophie," Mary whined at me lightly. "What are you going to do? Spend another night at home reading…" she reached into my open backpack and grabbed one of the books out. "The Short Stories of Henry James? Just the thought is making me fall asleep."

"There's nothing wrong with reading," I told her as I snatched the book from her hands. I placed my backpack on the floor and put the book back inside, making sure to clasp the bag closed this time.

"No, there's nothing wrong with reading at all," Mary retorted, "But you could spice things up a bit once in a while too. Maybe throw in a little Fifty Shades book now and then for good measure." She smiled wryly at me as she said this and I could feel my cheeks start to blush at the thought.

"You know I don't go in for trashy romance books Mary," I said as I tried to make my blushing cool down a bit faster.

"Well I like a little trashy now and then," she said as she twirled around a bit and laughed, causing her floral print skirt to spin open a bit.

"Who's talking about trashy?" I heard the voice echo down the hall as Mary and I turned quickly to see who it was.

"Oh geez," Mary groaned as she rolled her eyes at me. It was too late for us to make a quick break for the exit. It was Kenny Price, the school vice-principal ambling down the hallway towards us. Kenny, oddly enough, had started at the school the same time we had, but he looked as if he had aged ten times faster than we did. Even though he was the same age as us at thirty-two, his hairline was starting to recede and what was once a fit and toned body had softened quite a bit over the years. The cheesy, bushy, brown mustache he had had flecks of gray in it already too, earning him the nickname "The Walrus" with students and teachers alike.

Kenny stood before us, wearing khaki shorts and black dress socks with his loafers, and Mary and I had to do all we could to stifle laughter.

"Hi Kenny," I said. "Mary and I were just talking about books."

"Oh, that's too bad," Kenny said, hoping perhaps for a juicier story to latch on to. "So, what are you up to tonight Sophie? I was going to see what was playing at The Royal Theater tonight. Care to join me? We could go there and then to Stearn's for ice cream after."

Kenny had the hopeful twinkle in his eyes that he had every time he asked me out. I had gone out with him once or twice years ago when we first met but had been regularly rebuffing him since then when he tried to get a little too handsy for my tastes on the second date. He apologized back then, but he kept trying to get me to go out with him anyway.

"I'm sorry Kenny," I said, trying to sound sincere. "Mary and I already have plans to go out for dinner tonight."

The twinkle quickly disappeared at the rejection. "Okay, no problem," Kenny told me dejectedly, clearly feeling a bit embarrassed that I had turned him down in front of someone else. "You gals have a fun time tonight."

"Maybe another time, " I said to him apologetically.

"Sure thing," the hope returned to his face as he answered me before he turned and headed back down the hall towards the main office.

Mary hooked her arm around mine as she led me out the front doors towards the parking lot.

"Why do you do that to him?" Mary said to me.

"Do what?"

"Give him false hope about going out with you," she told me as we reached our cars, which just happened to be parked next to each other. "He had his shot with you. If he weren't a lecherous octopus, maybe things would have been different. Just the thought of him putting his hands on me.... Ewwww," Mary shook her body at the thought.

"I know," I told her as I put my backpack in the trunk of my car. "I guess I feel bad saying no all the time."

"Stop being so nice Sophie," Mary scolded me as she walked over to her car and climbed into the driver's seat. She rolled down the window to the passenger side of her car to talk to me. "Meet me at the Homestead at six?"

I sighed again. "I guess so," I said to her, knowing Henry James could wait another day.

"Great! Finally, a night out on the town with you. See you later!" Mary backed up and peeled out of the parking lot like she was one of the seniors in high school. I laughed as I waved away the dust she kicked up and climbed into the driver's seat of my trusty Camry.

As I slowly worked my way the long not-quite two miles from the school to my house on Hodges Avenue, I glanced over at the house on the corner of Collins Drive, right before my street. I always slowed down as I went passed, knowing it was his Dad's place. In my imagination, I half-expected to see him walk out the front door and stop me as I was going by, but of course, this never happened. Today was no different, though the house was clearly quieter now.

I wonder what will happen to the place, I considered as I kept driving by until I reached my driveway.

I pulled into the driveway and shut off my car, climbing out and grabbing my backpack from the trunk. I gave a casual wave to Mrs. Griffin, sitting out on her porch next door as she always does this time of day in the summer, and hopped up the steps of my porch to the front door. I checked the mailbox by the door before going in, and it was the usual junk mail.

Not even the mail is exciting in Canon, I thought to myself as I walked in the front door and tossed the mail on the end table.

I went into the kitchen, opened the fridge and got my pitcher of lemonade out and poured myself a glass. I walked over to the old rocker in the living room, the one I always sat in just like my mother did before me, and sat down to relax. It was only three-thirty, so I still had time before I had to meet Mary for dinner.

I picked up my backpack and held it in my hands. The brown leather had worn over the years, but the bag was still in great shape and had served me well. I ran my hand over the brass plate that had my initials on it, still visible after all this time, though with scratch marks and spots. I pulled the bag closer to me on my lap and closed my eyes, thinking back to the day I got the bag, the day he gave it to me as a gift, and how much I had smiled and loved it.

And loved him.

4

Travis

Abby and I had made pretty good progress on the road so far, getting to within about an hour of Canon after about two hours on the road. She had barely said three words to me since we got in the car. Instead she had slipped her earbuds in to listen to music while she frantically tapped away on her phone, chatting with someone and smiling along the way.

Finding a radio station once we got close to Canon was nearly impossible because of the mountains surrounding the area. Since I hadn't bothered to attach my phone to the car, I couldn't play any music I might like along the way, which left me to just get lost in my thoughts as I drove along. I took in the scenery as we went along the highway and was quickly reminded of how beautiful it was around here. The sun was still shining brightly, the trees looked beautiful, and the area around Canon was much more rural than what I had become accustomed to over the last several years.

We hadn't been back to Canon for a while to see my mom. In fact, it had been years since I had been here at all. Normally she would just get frustrated and come to see us in Ridgefield, constantly chiding me because I never came to see her. I certainly never went there to see my dad or anyone else for that matter. My parents had split up when I was seventeen, and even though they lived in the same town, I never saw him much, and even less after I left for college. I saw him once before Abby was born, and then talked to him on the phone after her birth, though it was more of a one-sided, drunken argument and chastising from him about how I threw my life away getting some girl pregnant. After that, I never spoke to him again, and never really wanted to.

My daydreaming continued on for a while, and before I knew it, I saw the sign for the exit for Canon and realized I had never called my mother to let her know we were coming. It was getting close to six, which meant she wasn't at home anymore and was already down at her place watching over everything for the dinner crowd. She had been running that restaurant for as long as I could remember, a business she inherited from her father and that she had operated with great pride, despite having to throw my father out of there more than once for drinking too much or getting cozy with one of the new waitresses. That's what eventually let her come to her senses and toss him out on his ear, permanently.

I had spent more than enough of my life at The Homestead. I spent hours there waiting for her while she worked and worked there as a busboy in high school. I didn't have much of a desire to go there at all tonight. I was tired, my leg hurt, my head hurt, and I didn't want to run into any old high school folks that I didn't want to see anyway.

"Dad," Abby said to me as she pulled the earbuds from her ears, "does Grandma know we're coming?"

"No, not really," I said to her as I turned off the exit ramp and headed out towards my mom's house on Wood Place.

"Then why are we going to her house? You know she won't be there. Let's just go to the restaurant."

"Honey," I sighed, "I've been driving for three hours, and I'm tired. I don't feel like dealing with the dinner crowd at the Homestead and trying to get Grandma's attention. We'll just go to the house, go in, and call her from there. She won't mind."

Wood Place was not far from the exit, and it was moments before we were pulling into the gravel driveway. The motion lights I had told her to get flipped on as we pulled in and I could hear Pee Wee, her St. Bernard, barking inside as soon as he heard us.

Abby bounded out of the car before the engine was off and scurried up the porch steps to the front door. I was barely out of the car, stretching my sore leg after the drive, and opening the trunk to get the bags when I saw the front door was open and Abby was inside. I didn't realize she was tall enough now to reach the broken shingle near the front door where my mom hid the spare key. She was growing up way too fast.

I grabbed our bags from the trunk and lumbered up the front steps of the porch and through the front doorway. The house looked and smelled the same as it did since the last time I was here, when Abby was a much smaller girl that needed me to carry her up the staircase to go to sleep. All the details were still the same, including the pictures in the hallway, the framed cross-stitch in the living room, and the old percolator that she refused to give up to make her coffee in the morning.

I dropped the bags in the hallway and sat down on the old leather couch in the living room and looked around. I flipped the light on next to the couch to brighten things up a bit, though the room was still a bit dark from the wood paneling in the room that Mom refused to replace. In a flash, Abby came racing around the corner with a giant, slobbering Pee Wee behind her. Abby threw herself onto the couch next to me, and Pee Wee immediately jumped up between us, practically knocking me off the couch with his head as he smiled a slobbering smile at me.

Abby praised him and petted him for a bit before he jumped down and lay on the floor in front of us. I was glad for the extra space and stretched out my legs a bit in front of me.

"Okay, let's go see Grandma," Abby said as she jumped up off the couch.

"I thought we already decided this," I told her, resisting her futile attempts to pull me up off the couch. "Let's just relax here and see her later."

"Well if you don't want to go, that's fine. I can walk down there myself."

Abby started walking towards the front door.

"Hold it," I shouted. Abby spun around on her heels and put her hands on her hips, immediately reminding me of the way her mother used to do the same thing.

"What?" she said as if she was itching for an argument.

"You're not walking there alone. It's getting dark."

"Dad, you can't be serious," she said to me incredulously. "I'm not a little kid anymore, and the restaurant is only a few blocks away. Besides, we're in Canon. They've already started rolling up the sidewalks."

She was, of course, right on all those points, and I didn't really feel like arguing with her.

"Fine, go, but make sure you have your phone with you," I told her, trying to sound as parental as possible.

"Thanks, Dad!" Abby yelled as she was out the door and down the porch steps.

I kicked back on the couch, swinging my sore leg up, and kicked my boots off onto the floor. I put my left arm over my eyes while my right dangled down on the floor and gently scratched behind Pee Wee's ear as we both rested. I closed my eyes, trying not to think too hard about anything at all – not the past, present, or future – and hoped I could get some peaceful sleep.

5

Sophie

I had dozed off in my rocking chair for much longer than I had anticipated. I woke with a start as I heard a car honk its horn as it went by the house, and I was already sorry I had woken up. I was still clutching the backpack in my arms and had been roused from a sweet dream, one I have every now and again. The two of us were there, back in college like we were years ago, but this time things didn't end as badly as they did. We stayed together, the outside world wasn't real, and there we were sitting on the front porch of our own place, watching the sun go down, holding hands. He leaned over and kissed me deeply, the way he always used to, still holding my hand. He then rose up from our front porch swing, pulled me by the hand and led me inside to the bedroom. Within moments the passion overtook both of us, and we were lying there together, blankets rumpled around us, clothing tossed aside, as we made love as the sun went down outside the window. It was intense and magical all at once, feeling him like that... feeling him in a way that I never had the chance to before.

And then that stupid horn went off and woke me up before anything else happened. Something always seemed to startle me up at just the wrong moment, and I never get to see how this dream plays out. I sat in the rocking chair for a moment, feeling flush all over, my body tingling from head to toe. I took a quick glance down at my watch and saw it was already six o'clock. Mary would think I was standing her up again and it would be moments before my cell phone was ringing or she was sending me a text to ask where I was.

I stood up from the rocker, tossing the backpack on the floor next to the chair as it creaked back and forth. I took a quick glance at myself in the mirror just inside my front door and fixed my hair a bit and pulled it back into a ponytail. As I was tightening my ponytail and tying it back with a piece of blue ribbon I had plucked from the top of the bureau, I took a closer look at myself. My face was still a bit flush, and even the top of my chest that was visible above the light blue dress I was wearing was a bit rosy as well.

That was some dream, I told myself as I picked up my purse and headed out the door.

I decided it was too nice of a night to drive over to The Homestead. Besides, it was only a few blocks away from here, like most things were in this small town, and there was rarely any parking on the street or in the small lot next to the restaurant anyway. I thought the walk would be good to help me clear my head a bit and help me build up my appetite for a night out. As I reached the corner of Collins Drive, I began to walk slowly passed the house. The house was dark, as it had been ever since his father passed away. I stood just outside the cyclone fence gate surrounding the front yard there and peered at the house. The porch paint was a bit worn, the gutter on the front of the house was hanging loose, and the front lawn was clearly in need of a mow. I could only imagine what the inside looked like if the outside had been let to go like this. I tried to get a glance through one of the front windows, the one where the shade was near all the way up, wondering if I could see anything inside. The only thing visible was an old chair positioned by the window. I couldn't make out much of the detail of it, but I remember it was where his father sat every day, reading with the window open while he played music on his record player or watched the ballgame so loud you could hear it from the street. I craned my neck to get a better look, peering closely, wanting to see something, and then received a jolt when I felt my phone buzz in my hand, making me jump back and drop my phone over the fence, onto the grass.

"Damn," I said lightly, as I now had to open the gate to get my phone.

At least Mary would be proud of me for swearing out loud, " I thought, making myself chuckle lightly. I opened the gate slowly, feeling some resistance from the rust on the hinges and as the gate tried to move through the overgrown grass. With the sun going down, it was a little darker on the lawn than I thought it would be and with the grass so high, finding my phone was not as easy as I thought it would be. I was finally able to locate it, and I glanced down, seeing the message from Mary –

"Where the hell are you? Don't stand me up again Sophie!"

I typed a quick message to her:

"On my way. Walking there right now."

I got up from my crouch and saw I was closer to the window now, but now that I was this close something inside me made me feel like the house didn't look so friendly now. It looked older, worn, almost sad. I found myself wanting to get out of there faster, and as I was looking at the house, I thought I could see a shadow inside by the window. I gasped audibly and stumbled, bumping into the gate as I turned, fumbled with the gate, and got it open so I could get out of there.

I raced down the street, not sure if I really saw something or if my imagination was just getting the better of me at this point with all my daydreaming today. I wasn't taking any chances and found myself moving quickly across the few blocks until I was outside the door to The Homestead in no time at all.

I opened the glass door to the entrance and went right inside. There was no one stationed at the hostess podium, where Maggie could almost always be found, and I was kind of glad about that today. I was feeling a bit out of breath as I scanned the room quickly, hoping to spot Mary. I saw her seated at a table near the center of the room, a drink in her hand as she smirked and waved at me.

The dining room was a decent size since this was the only restaurant of note in town, with about fifteen or twenty tables of various sizes, but every table was already filled, and all the seats at the large mahogany bar along the far end of the room were all taken as well. There were TVs on by the bar, but Maggie always made them keep the sound muted because she didn't want to disturb the dining patrons. I plopped myself down in the wooden chair opposite where Mary was sitting and watched her take another sip of her drink, finishing it off.

"Where were you? You're late," she chided me as she set her glass down. "Are you okay? You look flushed."

I took a deep breath to further compose myself. Now I wasn't sure if I was flush from the experience at the house, my dream or what.

"I'm fine," I told her as I brushed the hair out of my face. It was just then that I noticed that I had lost my ribbon somewhere along the way. " I ran over here so I could meet you without being too late. You don't happen to have a hair tie, do you? I seem to have lost mine."

Mary looked at me and then pointed at her recently cut short auburn hair. "Remember, my haircut two weeks ago? I've been complaining about it ever since I got it cut at Gail's place. I never should have let that blonde butcher my hair." She ran her right hand over the short length as she spoke to emphasize her anger over it.

"Sorry, I forgot about that," I told her sincerely, brushing the hair from my eyes again.

"I have a hair tie you can use Ms. Ingram," a voice said to my side. I looked up and saw our server, Patty Watkins, a former student of mine who was now a senior in the high school and worked at the restaurant. She was looking more grown-up than ever, making me feel old again as I saw her in her crisp white blouse and black slacks, with her own blonde hair pulled back. She reached into her apron and pulled out a small black hair tie and handed it to me.

"Oh thank you, Patty, that's very sweet of you," I said to her as I tied my hair back into its ponytail.

"No problem, Ms. Ingram," she said to me with a smile. "Can I get you something to drink?"

"I'll just have a lemonade Patty, please," I told her as I watched her scribble it down on her pad.

"Another cosmo for you Ms. Connors?" Patty asked with a smile.

"You bet Patty, thanks for asking," Mary said as she handed Patty her empty glass. Patty walked away, laughing lightly to herself as she headed towards the bar to place the drink order.

"Lemonade? Really, Sophie? We're supposed to be out having fun tonight, and you order lemonade to drink. No wonder everyone thinks you're a spinster."

Mary sat back and smiled at me.

"Who says I'm a spinster?" I said indignantly.

"More than one person, Sophie. It's a small town, remember? Word gets around pretty quickly. When is the last time you actually went out on a date? And I mean with someone besides me?"

I had to think hard how to answer that question. It had been long enough where I couldn't really remember when it was.

"There was that substitute English teacher I went to the poetry reading with," I said to her proudly.

"Sophie, that guy hasn't been around here for three years, and you only went out with him that one time. Face it, it has been a long time. It has been too long. I don't know how you do it. I couldn't go this long without ever being with a man."

My face blushed deep red when Mary said it. "Mary! Could you say it a little louder? I don't think the guys in the kitchen heard you." I was suddenly feeling very warm, and of course, Patty, who was in earshot, arrived with our drinks, making me blush even more. She handed me my lemonade and Mary her cosmo.

"If you're looking for a date Ms. Ingram, my dad is single again. I'm sure I could fix you up," Patty said with a smile.

I groaned audibly and wished the chair I was in would swallow me whole. Seventeen-year-olds were now going to be clued in on my virgin status and looking to set me up with their eligible fathers by lunchtime tomorrow.

"Thanks but no, Patty," I said to her quietly. "Can we just order dinner, Mary?" I said to Mary through my gritted teeth.

We both quickly ordered The Homestead hamburgers and their fresh-cut french fries, hoping to get Patty to move along quickly. Patty took the order and left, feeling a bit sheepish.

"I'm sorry about that Sophie," Mary said to me sincerely. "You know I didn't mean to embarrass you like that. I just worry about you, that's all." She held her glass towards me across the table. I reached for my lemonade, smiled at her, and we clinked our glasses together.

We chatted idly for a while, covering all the local gossip as we watched most of the town gather and come and go out of the restaurant. Everyone pretty much dined here, drank here, or got takeout from here, so it was pretty common to see everyone and anyone here, whether you wanted to or not.

Our burgers came out, cooked perfectly, and Mary and I both attacked ours with fervor. We laughed and giggled like high school girls, and for the first time in a long time I was glad she had dragged me out of my shell a bit and out into public.

As we finished our meals, I saw Maggie for the first time tonight as she came out of the kitchen. She had her back to us as she walked backward towards us, and she was clearly talking to someone in front of her, but I couldn't see who. It was then that I saw it was a girl, not quite as tall as Maggie but close, with long red hair. She looked a lot like many of the girls I see in my eighth-grade class, but I had never seen her around here before. The girl was laughing and smiling at Maggie and talking very animatedly, waving her hands around as she spoke. I saw the girl hand her phone to one of the other servers in the restaurant, and she then placed her arm around Maggie's waist as the two of them posed for a picture together. The flash from the camera on the phone blinded me briefly, and I blinked hard several times to regain focus. It was then that I got a better look at the girl and saw that she had marvelous emerald green eyes. They were eyes that I had seen once before; eyes that you don't forget easily.

There was no doubt in my mind – they were his eyes.

6

Travis

It was another restless sleep with fitful dreams. I can never seem to escape the dreams of the fire and losing my friend, but being back home in Canon clearly triggered other things in mind. I could see myself back in this house as a young boy, listening to my mother and father have their usual arguments about how he drank too much, spent too much and fooled around too much and how my father would spit back at my mother in his spiteful, mean tone about how no one else would want her and how he deserved better. I would just stand behind the door when I was eight or nine and just listen, fearful about the violence that could break out at any moment.

My dream then flashed forward to when I was seventeen, and I would occasionally go over to my father's house to see him. He would be sitting in that chair by the window, sometimes already drunk by early afternoon, sometimes just sitting there lost in his own world. More often than not he never responded to what I would ask, and when he did it was rarely something nice. Even in my dreams, he was just as mean and just as hurtful, and I stood there and took it.

Flash again to college, when I finally got away from Canon and got the chance to be happy. Going around campus, making new friends, meeting new people, and finally getting to be with her, and just her. I could see us in my dream, sitting there outside by the quad, laughing, holding each other and just getting lost in her blue eyes. Just as suddenly as it had started, the dream seemed to end, and she was pulled away from me and was gone. I was reaching for her, trying to pull her back to me, and I saw her slipping away just like everything else has always done in my life to now.

The slam of the screen door on the porch caused me to jump awake on the couch. It took me a few seconds to catch my breath and realize where I was now, and then I saw Abby walk through the door smiling, with my mother following closely behind her. I glanced down at my watch, the one the guys at the fire company gave me while I was recuperating in the hospital, and saw it was nearly 11 PM.

"Hey Dad," Abby said to me as she bounded over towards me and knelt on the floor to pet Pee Wee, who immediately rolled over onto his belly for her. "You missed a great time at The Homestead. I had a great burger while I was there, and a mountain of fries too." She licked her lips just at the thought of what she had eaten.

My mother walked over and stood next to where Abby was kneeling. Not much had changed since the last time I had seen her when she came to visit us about six months ago. Her auburn hair had a few more flecks of gray in it, but she looked just as strong as she always had and stood tall as she looked down at me sitting on the couch.

"I brought a burger back for you if you're hungry, " she said to me, holding up a white plastic bag from the restaurant.

"Thanks, Mom," I said to her as I stood up slowly from the couch, shaking the cobwebs from my head and the stiffness in my leg. I gave her a peck on the cheek as I stretched, standing next to her.

"Abby, you need to get to bed," I said to her. "It's getting late."

"Why?" she said to me with a slight whine. "It's not like I have school tomorrow or anything. I want to hang out for a while." She sat on the floor, crossing her arms defiantly as she glared at me.

"Come on Abs," my mother said to her sweetly. "You can have the room next to mine. Your Dad can take his old room. I'll help you get set up."

Abby readily went along with my mother's suggestions, like it was a much better idea than what I had just suggested. Abby stood up and came over and gave me a hug. "Goodnight Dad," she said to me sweetly as she squeezed me tight.

"Goodnight honey," I told her as I squeezed her back and gave her a kiss on the top of her head. Abby broke the hug and went over and grabbed her bag from the hallway and started up the stairs.

My mother handed me the plastic bag of food. "Why don't you go in the kitchen and eat. I'll get her settled and come down in a minute." She strode toward the stairs and smiled at me as she worked her way up, following Abby.

I took the bag into the kitchen and sat myself down at the small, square wooden table in the kitchen. The kitchen itself did not look that much different from the last time I saw it, or from the years before that. My mom was never much of one for decorating or big furnishings. I think she figured she spent so much time out of the house that there really wasn't much of a need for fancy stuff at home. She always had just what we needed – nothing less, nothing more.

I opened up the plastic bag and took the white, styrofoam box out. I went over to the fridge to see what there was to drink, which wasn't much. There was some milk, a half pitcher of iced tea, and another half pitcher of lemonade. Mom always did like her Arnold Palmer. As much as I would have liked to have a cold beer, there wasn't much of a chance of finding one in here. Mom never drank much outside of the occasional glass of wine, and never kept beer around because Dad always drank it all. Even after she tossed him out, there was never beer here.

As I closed the refrigerator door, Mom walked into the kitchen.

"I would have brought you some beer if I knew you were coming," she said to me in that tone all mothers seem to have when they are not quite scolding their children.

"I'm sorry about that," I said to her sincerely. "It was a last-minute decision to come."
"Well, you do have a cell phone right? I mean even I have a cell phone," as she took her phone out of the pocket of her black trousers and waved at me, half-mocking me.

"Yes, I do. I'm sorry. I should have called." I sat down at the table and opened the styrofoam box to start in on my hamburger. Once I started eating, I realized just how hungry I was and ate the hamburger ravenously, eating more than half of it in just a few bites.

"You always had good burgers down there," I said to Mom as I wiped juice from the burger that I had dripped onto my chin with the back of my hand.

"Oh Travis, use a napkin for heaven's sake," she said to me as she grabbed a napkin off the counter and handed it to me. I finished wiping my chin and then my hand with the napkin and smiled at her as I took another bite of burger.

Mom sat down at the table across from me and looked at me seriously.

"Why are you here Travis?" she asked. "You haven't come to my house in years. I was beginning to think you forgot how to drive to Canon."

It was the same thing she said every time she came down to see Abby and me.

"That lawyer keeps calling me about Dad," I said to her as I finished the last of the burger.

"Who? Irv Rogers? What does he want?"

"I don't know," I told her as I sat back in the wooden chair, still tasting the last of the burger on my lips. "He said I had papers to sign about Dad's estate."

"Estate," she said with a cough and a laugh. "Your father barely had a pot to piss in, pardon my French."

It was always funny to hear her swear, even though at times she swore like a truck driver.

"Well he must have had something he didn't hock or pawn," I said to her.

"He did," Mom said as she got up and poured two glasses of iced tea, handing one to me. She sat back down across the table from me. "He had that house."

I was surprised by what she said. "Dad owned that place? I thought he was just renting it all that time."

"No," she said to me with a sigh and then she took a long sip of iced tea. "I bought that house for him when I threw him out. I paid for it outright in cash and bought it from Mr. Watson."

"Why did you buy him a house?" I couldn't believe what I was hearing.

"Because it was the only way I could get him to agree to leave me and sign the divorce papers without him asking for part of the restaurant, and I wasn't going to let that happen. I worked too hard for that place. So I bought the house, put it in his name and gave him the keys after he signed the papers."

"How come you never told me about it before?" I asked her.

"I never thought it was important I guess," she said. "I always figured he would end up selling it for the cash somewhere along the way. I think he held onto it in spite more than anything else. Like it was hurting me because he got something out of me."

"Well, what I am supposed to do with it?" I asked her. All of a sudden I was a homeowner, whether I liked it or not.

"That's up to you," she said. She got up from the table, grabbing my trash and tossed it in the garbage can in the corner. "God only knows what kind of shape it's in. I don't know when the last time was that you saw your father, but he rarely left that house before he had that heart attack."

I felt a tinge of guilt for not seeing him for so long. Even though he was far from a nice guy to Mom or me, he was still my father.

Mom came over and put her hand on my shoulder.

"Don't feel bad about it honey," she said as she patted my shoulder in comfort. "We both know how he really was. He doesn't deserve your guilt or your sympathy. He brought on his own pain by living the way he did. Nothing you could have done would have changed that. Besides, you have more important things to think about. You need to take care of that granddaughter of mine."

"It becomes more of a challenge with each passing day Mom," I told her, feeling exasperated.

"It doesn't get easier as they get older, Travis, trust me. I still worry about you every day."

"You don't need to worry about me, Mom. I'm fine. We're fine." I said it just as much to reassure myself as I did her.

"That doesn't mean I'm going to stop worrying. A young man raising an almost-teenage daughter on his own with no woman in sight. And you're a firefighter to boot as if there weren't enough worries. It pretty much keeps me up at night."

"I think my firefighting days might be over," I said to her resignedly. "I don't think there's much of a chance they would take me back. With my injury I don't how much good I would be anyway. The department already sent me my retirement papers. I just have to sign them."

"Oh Travis, I'm sorry." Mom bent down and hugged me around my neck. "Well, maybe all this is a blessing in disguise. You and Abby can finally get out of that tiny rented place you have and have a house of your own."

"You mean live back here in Canon? I don't know Mom. I don't know if I could do it. There's too much... too much history here." The thought of spending my days back here in Canon was scary.

"You can't just think about yourself, Travis," she said as she stood back up. "You have to do what's right for Abby at this point. Sometimes being a parent has to trump the decisions we would make just for ourselves."

I know she was talking about what she did back when I was a teenager. I am sure she sacrificed all her savings to buy that house for Dad and had to work twice as hard to make up for it over the last fifteen years. She did it so that I could have a better life, a safer life without him around every day.

"I know," I told her as I stood up from the chair and hugged her tightly. "I promise I'll consider it after I have a look at the house."

"Fair enough," she said to me as we broke our hug. She looked up at me, her eyes a little cloudy with tears. "it's wonderful to have you here, you know; To have the both of you here. It means a lot to me."

"Oh don't go getting all mushy on me, Mom," I said to her playfully as I moved out of the kitchen and out into the hall to get my bag.

"Do you remember where your room is?" she shouted to me playfully.

"I think I can find it," I told her as I picked up my bag and moved towards the stairs. "Goodnight Mom," I told her as I started up the stairs slowly.

My leg ached some as I made it to the top of the stairs. I tried to walk down the hall towards the room where Abby was quietly, but the floorboards didn't cooperate and creaked the entire way. I peered into the room to see Abby scrunched up under the blanket on the bed, already fast asleep. I smiled as I looked in at her, sleeping peacefully, with a hint of a smile on her face. It was nice to see her so happy for a change.

I slowly closed the door and went down to the opposite end of the hall to my old room. I reached in and flipped the light switch, and the room illuminated, revealing to me the room that was pretty much the same as it was the last time I was in it when I was about twenty. The room was plainly decorated, with just a dresser, a small desk and chair and a full-sized bed in the center of the room. Anything that had been on the shelves Mom had long since packed away or tossed out. The bed was made up like Mom was expecting me at any moment, and I placed my bag on the chair for the desk and sat on the bed.

I realized the last time I was in here was when I came home to drop the bombshell news on my mother. I came to tell her I had passed the firefighter's exam and had gotten a girl pregnant. It wasn't at all what she had hoped to hear from me, and it was far from easy for me to lay all of that at her feet, but she took it all in stride. We didn't even argue much about it, as she told me I was a man old enough to find my own path in life now. She was a little disappointed about the pregnancy since it was with a girl she didn't know and one I barely knew, but the prospect of being a grandmother was appealing to her.

I am sure she had hoped that relationship would work out for me, but I guess neither one of us saw what was coming with all that. In the end, even though Brenda up and left me without warning with a two-month-old little girl, it was for the best. I got and still have Abby out of all of it, and Abby got my mother to be with and learn from over the years.

I pushed myself off the bed and decided to hang a couple of things in my closet. I grabbed a couple of my shirts and pairs of jeans and opened the closet door. Nothing was hanging in there at the moment, but the shelves were filled with some boxes. I saw in the corner of the shelf an old shoebox, the one I had always kept some mementos in during my younger days. I reached over and grabbed it off the shelf and opened it up.

There wasn't much left inside there. There were a few medals I had won in high school as part of the wrestling team, a couple of flattened coins I had gotten from the train tracks in town, and my old learner's permit from when I first learned how to drive. There were also a couple of pictures in the box. One was of Mom, Dad and I in front of the Christmas tree. I looked to be about seven or eight, and it was probably one of the few times all three of us were smiling at the same time. I was standing between Mom and Dad, and the three of us had our hands on the bike I had just gotten for Christmas. The bike served me well for years when I wanted to go anywhere with friends or just escape when Dad had wandered home drunk.

The other picture inside had me sit back down on the bed. It was a picture from my college years, one I had forgotten about. There I was, with my arm around Sophie, the both of us beaming with pride as we had just gotten back to Canon after our freshman year at school. The picture was taken outside the front steps of my Mom's house.

I don't know if I had forgotten just how beautiful she was, or if I tried to put it out of my memory because it was too painful for me, but seeing her in that picture brought it all flooding back. I put the pictures back in the box, closed the lid, and put the box on the dresser. I laid back on the bed, staring up at the white ceiling, seeing the same spots I had seen years before. I felt myself drifting off to sleep again, thinking about what the future might hold for me, for Abby, for us.

7

Sophie

I spent the entire rest of the evening feeling distracted. I couldn't get the girl out of my mind – all through dessert, paying the check and leaving the Homestead. Even the ride home with Mary, who graciously offered to drive me the few blocks, so I didn't have to walk back in the dark, was just a blur. I do remember her asking me why I was so distracted, but I can't even recall what I said to her. I got out of the car and mindlessly walked into my house, putting myself in the rocking chair and gently rocking back and forth as I tried to figure it out.

While the girl had red hair, which was nothing like what Travis had or his mother or father had, there was no denying she had his eyes. As I looked at her, I could see features in her face that reminded me of him – the slope of her jaw, the pert nose she had, even the way she smiled – it all seemed to be like him. Maybe I just wanted to see it in her because I had been thinking about him so much lately, but it was more than that. The way she hugged Maggie and put her arm around her, there was definite familiarity there. While I couldn't be sure, I had to assume they were related in some way. Travis had no siblings, so it wasn't a niece of his. Perhaps a relative I didn't know about?

I must have sat in that chair for hours trying to figure it out. I even pulled out old photo albums, ones my mother had saved from when I was younger, and pictures I had from college. It had been a long time since I had looked at those pictures, mainly because it was painful for me to look at them. When I see them I am reminded of how happy we were, how much in love I was with him and how much he cared for me, and how it all came crashing down so suddenly and then he was gone from my life. There were pictures of us at parties, hanging out with friends, and even pictures of us when we came back to Canon after that first year. When I compared them to what I saw tonight, it was hard to believe that she couldn't be his daughter.

I scanned back to pictures of when I was young. Travis and I knew each other all through school; it is a very small town after all. We were friends when we were younger, but we didn't hang out much. He was into sports and had his friends, I was into studying and clubs and had mine. We didn't even date in the same circles, and I had no idea how he felt about me until we met up at college. At first, we clung to each other more because we were the only people we knew so far away from home, but over time, as we became better friends, it turned into something more. Then there was that party we went to one weekend where Travis had a bit more to drink than he probably should have and told me that he had always felt something for me, all through high school, but he never worked up the nerve to say anything to me. I was stunned when he told me. I figured this big, strong guy in high school was not going to even take notice of a bookworm like me. I wasn't mousy, but I kept to myself, much like I do now. I didn't go out much even with friends and dated even less. My mother was the proverbial double-edged sword with me – she wanted me to go out and meet people, but she kept telling me how important it was that I take care of myself and not get swept off my feet by some guy who just wanted to have sex with me. I took all that heart, which is partly why I was still a virgin at thirty-two.

It's not that I didn't ever want to have sex. There were many times with Travis where we came achingly close. More than once we were fooling around in the back of his car or in his dorm room when his roommate wasn't around. I can remember getting all hot and bothered, kissing him deeply, feeling his hands on me, touching me intimately over and under my clothes. When it came down to actually making love with him, I just felt I wasn't ready for it. I knew I loved him, but something always held me back from giving myself over. Travis, as frustrated as he would get at times, was always respectful and never pushed himself on me, which I think made me love him even more then and now.

I knew I was not going to be able to let this go. Even as I got myself ready for bed, putting on my ratty old gray t-shirt and gray cotton sleep shorts, I was trying to decide what to do. I could go over to Maggie's house in the morning, see who is there, and just find out for myself. As good as that sounded, I was too afraid for an abrupt run-in with Travis. What if he was there with his daughter and… his wife? Clearly, if there was a daughter, he was married. Travis was nothing if not loyal and dedicated, and I could not deal with the immediate feelings that would cause for me.

It was then I got a better idea. The Homestead was always open for lunch, and Maggie was always there at lunchtime, either at the hostess podium or working the dining room and getting things ready for the dinner crowd. The place wasn't nearly as busy for lunch as dinner since more people were at work, and maybe I could get some time to talk to her, get some information, and see what was going on.

I snuggled back into my pillow feeling proud of myself for coming up with that idea. I tried to close my eyes and get right to sleep, but the nervousness and excitement that filled me were probably a bit more than I could bear. I wasn't sure what I was hoping for or how I would handle what I learned, but for the first time in a long time, I felt a warmness in my heart that made me genuinely happy.

8

Sophie

Morning came faster than I thought it would, and while my body felt tired because I spent most of the night wondering how the meeting with Maggie would go, I had the energy to get moving. It was actually later than I had slept in a while since I had been getting up early, prepping myself for the school day mornings that were not far off, and going into my classroom to get everything ready for the new year. Luckily, I didn't actually have to be there on these days; it was more of a voluntary thing to help me get ahead. The extra time allowed me to spend more time than I might usually have spent getting myself ready for the day. I found myself staring at my closet, trying to pick out my prettiest dress, and I was kind of disappointed by what I saw there. It was then I realized that I hadn't done much pampering of myself in a long while and my wardrobe showed it. Everything looked just like you would expect an eighth-grade schoolteacher to dress – conservative, bland, without much flair and color. I was starting to see more of why people thought I was a spinster. All I needed was three or four cats roaming around, and I was all set.

I finally found something pushed to the far side of my closet that I thought looked breezy and perfect for summer. It was a casual tank dress, sleeveless, and a light yellow. It was knee-length and flared out a bit to make the dress look light and feel comfortable. I had bought the dress about a year ago at Simmons, our local clothing store, but I hadn't worn it since then.

Now is as good a time as any, Sophie, I told myself and laid the dress on the bed.

I took a long, leisurely, hot shower, and after wrapping a fluffy, white towel around myself, I walked over to the mirror over my vanity and took a look at myself. I thought about putting some makeup on, but I rarely wore any and I opted to skip it. I did blow-dry my hair, however, something I rarely did except on cold mornings before school. Drying and brushing out my hair took a bit longer than I thought it would, and I realized my hair had gotten quite a bit longer since the last time I got it cut. I would usually go and get it done right before school started, and had to remember to do that. Today, however, I was putting the school out of my head.

I slipped into my basic white cotton bra and panties and then pulled the dress on over my head. I looked over in the mirror and was very happy with how it looked on me. I actually felt good wearing it instead of my usual clothes, and I spun around a little in front of the mirror to make the dress twirl a bit as I smiled at my reflection. I put my watch on and realized it was almost 11:30, still a little early for lunch, but I wanted to get there and have time to talk to Maggie without fear of getting interrupted. I slipped into my slip-on sneakers and moved down the stairs. I picked up my purse, checked myself in the mirror one last time, and headed out the door.

It was already feeling warm out, not at all unusual for late August around here. The sun beat down brightly, and the neighborhood kids were all running around under a sprinkler two houses down from me. I thought about walking to The Homestead again, but then remembered I would have to walk by the house again. Something about doing that scared me off a bit, so I got my keys out and opted to go with the short drive instead.

I turned the air conditioning up as soon as I turned the car on to get it working as soon as possible. I knew it seemed silly to do that for just a few minutes I would be in the car, but I felt like between the heat and the bit of nervousness I felt that the last thing I wanted to be was a sweaty mess before I got there. I pulled out of my driveway and was on my way. I drove slowly past Travis' father's house as I went by, taking a quick glance at it to see if it was still intent on menacing me somehow. The house looked more rundown in the sunshine, like it had lacked love and attention for a long time. I eased my foot on the gas to speed past it a bit so I could put it out of my mind.

In no time at all, I was turning into the parking lot next to the restaurant. There were just a few cars in the lot, as I expected. I turned my car off and started to get out when I found myself struck with a thought.

What if Travis is in there?

I'm not sure why I hadn't considered that a possibility before, but it certainly could happen. That knot in my stomach started to tighten more, and I could feel myself gripping the door handle but not opening it. The thought that Travis could be in there, having a happy lunch with his wife and daughter, laughing and smiling, was gutwrenching, to say the least. I could just as easily turn the car back on and go home, forget about all of this, and go on with my life.

Sure you can, the voice in my head said to me. *While you're at it, drive over to the animal shelter and pick up your cats, because that is where you are headed.*

I exhaled deeply, opened the car door, and got out. I could feel my legs shaking a little as I took the short walk through the parking lot and onto the sidewalk before I reached the front door of the restaurant. I peered in through the glass briefly and didn't see Maggie at the podium. She wouldn't not be here for lunch; that wasn't her.

Of course, she might not be here. Her granddaughter, son, and daughter-in-law are in town, and she wants to spend time with them. Get back in the car; your cats are waiting for you.

"No!" I said out loud, startling the two older women walking past me on the sidewalk. I blushed as they went by me. I was sure they would be telling everyone they knew how the school's eighth-grade spinster English teacher is now talking to herself as well.

My sudden burst of bravery got the better of me, and I pulled the glass door open and walked inside. The blast of cool air from the air conditioning made goosebumps stand up all over my body, and I felt myself shiver. I peered past the podium and saw just one or two people seated in the restaurant eating or ordering lunch. One of the waitresses, a teenager with brown hair snapping gum in her teeth, who I did not recognize, walked over to me.

"Would you like a table?" she asked me, popping her gum.

"Um... I guess.. is Maggie here?" I asked her awkwardly.

"Oh yeah, she's here. She's behind the bar. The afternoon bartender called in sick, but I don't think he's sick. A little too much partying last night for him, if you know what I mean." The girl winked at me and smiled. It was more information than I wanted.

"Yes," I said to her, hoping to cut off the conversation. "I'll ... I'll just go sit at the bar if that's alright."

"Sure," she said to me, chomping on her gum again. "Suit yourself." She turned and walked towards the kitchen as I made my way towards the bar.

To be honest, I don't think I had ever sat at the bar here before. It's not that I don't drink, I just rarely have any alcohol. One bad experience in college with some tequila was more than I needed to set me straight. Now it was the very rare glass of wine, and that was about it.

I sat at a stool in the middle of the bar. I could feel the cold vinyl of the stool come right through the thin material of my dress, making me shiver once again. My feet didn't reach the floor sitting here at the bar, and I suddenly felt like I was twelve years old and doing something I shouldn't be doing. One other person was sitting at the bar, a few seats down from me. I recognized him as Fred Perkins, the owner of the dry cleaner shop down the street. He was a friendly man, always with a nice smile whether you saw him inside or outside the store. I wondered why he would be here early during the week instead of at his shop.

I found out shortly when I saw Maggie emerge from the door at the far end of the bar that led to a backroom. Fred perked up and beamed at her as she came in, blushing the same way I have seen many adolescent boys do in my classroom when the girl they like happens to walk by. Maggie stopped off for a moment to talk to Fred, leaning over the bar closely to him as she gently laughed and took his lunch order. She turned to the right and saw me sitting there, and a surprised look came over her face. She excused herself from Fred and made her way down to me.

"Sophie? I'm surprised to see you here so early. And sitting at the bar too. What's up?"

"Oh, I just decided to skip the classroom today and treat myself to an early lunch," I said to her, trying to sound casual.

"Good for you," she said enthusiastically. She handed me a menu to look at. I wasn't really that hungry, especially with my stomach doing backflips with knots, but now that I had told her I was here for lunch, I needed to order something.

"I'll have the Cobb salad, with the house dressing," I said to her, picking the first thing I saw. I wasn't even sure if I really liked Cobb salad, or exactly what was in it, but since today was a day of taking chances, I figured what the heck.

"Anything to drink?" she asked me. I thought about ordering a real drink, but my senses got the better of me.

"Just a lemonade," I said to her, feeling a bit embarrassed. There was that adolescent feeling again!

"No problem honey," she said to me. She stopped a few steps down the bar to pour a beer from the tap for Fred, and then went down and placed it in front of him, smiling (or was it flirting?) at him. She then turned to her register, entered what I assumed was my order, and disappeared into the backroom again.

I felt my legs swinging nervously, and I could feel myself spinning the stool lightly as I waited. The wait seemed endless to me, and the restaurant was almost unbearably quiet. I glanced up at the muted TV to see the sports news scrolling something about someone's knee injury. Maggie came back out and brought Fred his lunch, a hamburger with fries, and slid the plate in from of him. Fred thanked her profusely as she then made her way down to me with my tall glass of lemonade.

"One fresh lemonade," she said as reached down and grabbed a straw. "I just made it myself."

"Thanks, Maggie," I said to her, trying not to show my nervousness to her. I took a sip of the tart lemonade and felt it hit the back of my throat as it went down, making me choke a little.

"Easy, sweetie," Maggie said to me. "That's strong stuff you know."

I could feel myself turning red again as she smiled at me and went back down towards Fred. He had already finished most of his burger and was trying to engaging Maggie in conversation when I heard a cell phone ring. It was obviously Fred's, as he pulled it from his shirt pocket and flipped it open, disappointed that his conversation was interrupted. He had a brief, animated discussion with whoever was on the phone with him, hung up angrily, and sat back down with his shoulders slumped. He told Maggie he had to go, there was some problem with someone misplacing Mrs. Henderson's favorite dress, and she was ranting and raving in the shop. Maggie reached over and touched his hand gently and said it was okay, causing him to brighten with a smile again. He took money out of his wallet and left it on the bar, turned and smiled at me widely as he walked out, obviously happy with how things went.

Good for you Mr. Perkins.

Maggie had disappeared again, but quickly came bouncing back with my lunch. As she was putting the plate in front of me, I knew it was now or never time for me. I took a quick glance down at the salad, which looked yummy with its chicken, hard-boiled egg, bacon, and avocado with some bleu cheese crumbles over greens. I lightly picked at the salad as

Maggie took some glassware out of the dishwasher behind the bar to my left.

"So Maggie," I began, hearing my voice cracking slightly as I spoke, " Mary and I were in here last night. It was pretty busy."

"Yes, I was surprised it was so packed for a Thursday night. But you know, summer, small town, it's hot, no one wants to cook. It's all good for me," she said with a laugh.

"Yeah, I guess it is," I could feel the nervousness making it's way from my stomach up to my throat, trying to cut me off. I had to get it out before I stopped myself.

"I saw you in here, with a young girl, a redhead," I said as I grabbed a forkful of greens and shoved them into my mouth.

"Oh?" Maggie said to me. There was a slight twinkle in her eye as she closed the dishwasher and came closer to me.

I swallowed my greens slowly, trying not to choke. "Yes," I said, feeling my hand tremble a little as I pierced a piece of chicken. "I had never seen her before. She looked like she would be the age of the girls in my class. I was just wondering who she was." There, I had said it. It was hanging out there, and I just had to brace myself for the reply.

Maggie put her arms on the bar in front of me. "That was my granddaughter, Abby," she told me. A seriousness came over her face as she said it, making me feel like I had to brace for the worst news I could hear. That knot was in my throat now, and I could almost feel tears welling up in my eyes.

"Granddaughter," I said solemnly, trying to look like it didn't bother me. "So... so Travis has a daughter." I am sure

Maggie could tell this was tearing me up inside, but I had to press on. "I'm sure he and... and his wife... are very proud. She's a very pretty girl." I forced myself to take a bite of avocado, though now it felt like acid going down my throat. I washed it down with some lemonade, which made me cough and choke again. I grabbed my napkin and coughed into it, using it to wipe the light tears I could feel in my eyes.

I felt Maggie's hands pull mine down slowly from my face. She could see my eyes were red now, and I tried to hold myself back from bawling. I could see her smiling at me.

"Travis isn't married, Sophie," she said to me, using the napkin I was holding to wipe my face.

"He's not?" I said to her, finding it hard to believe the Travis would divorce anyone.

"Nope never has been," Maggie told me. "Brenda, Abby's mother, took off when she was two months old. She didn't want a family or to be tied down. She wanted to live a "free" life. Travis hasn't seen or heard from her since. He's raised Abby by himself... well, with a little help from me along the way," she said proudly.

I felt a huge weight lifted off me as the knot went away. I laughed a little as the last tear fell, and took another bite of my salad. Suddenly, Cobb salad tasted like the best thing I had ever eaten.

I took a quick glance down at my watch to feign interest in it.

"Oh, look at what time it is," I said in haste, trying to move quickly. "I need to get over to the school for paperwork." I fumbled with my purse, trying to get it open.

"I thought you said you were skipping school today," Maggie said to me, arching an eyebrow.

"I did, I mean I was going to, but I really should get some work in. Classes start in just a few weeks." I pulled my wallet out of my purse. "What do I owe you?" I asked Maggie.

"No charge," Maggie told me as I tried to hand her a twenty. "Lunch is on me. Just two friends getting together for a little catching up, okay?"

I smiled broadly at her, maybe even wider than Fred Perkins had. "Thank you," I said to her softly.

"Your welcome Sophie," she said. "Come around again soon, okay?"

"I... I will. I promise," I told her as I practically skipped out of the restaurant.

I barely noticed the wave of heat that hit me as I walked outside and quick-stepped to my car. I opened the car door, sat down, turned the car on and felt warm air rush from the vents as it worked to get cool. I banged my palms on the steering wheel as I felt a huge grin on my face.

"You can forget about those cats," I said out loud to myself as I backed out and started driving over to the school, hoping to catch Mary there so I could tell her all about this.

9

Travis

At some point, mornings aren't going to feel like they come too soon. Lately, every morning comes after a terrible night of sleep. There's always one dream or another making my nights miserable. Last night it wasn't the dreams so much, though those moments certainly came up as well. Fitful images of my Dad, his house and trying to make my way through that mess were certainly part of it. I also had plenty of visions of Sophie, both good and bad. Sleeping on the old full-sized bed in my bedroom at my mother's certainly didn't help things. I wondered how I was able to sleep in this all those years ago. Granted I was bigger now than I was then, thanks to years of working out, training, and working at the firehouse. Still, this bed had plenty of dips and lumps so I could feel practically every spring poking me in the back all night long.

The sun peeked through the thin white curtain on the window much earlier than I had anticipated it and tried as I did to roll over and block it out, it just wasn't happening. I rolled back over and looked at my watch that I had placed on the rickety nightstand and saw it was barely 7 AM. I didn't have to get to Mr. Rogers office until 9 AM or so, so I had some time to shower, wake myself up some more and get ready for whatever this meeting was going to present to me.

I wandered down to the bathroom with my toiletries in tow and went in so I could shower. The bathroom, much like my bedroom, looked like it hadn't aged much since my teenage years. Everything was clean and in place, and Mom had even put in a new showerhead in the shower so that the flow was better than I ever remember it being when I was younger.

The hot water felt good on my skin and even helped to take some of the aches out of muscles and my leg. I took a quick look down at my leg as I showered. It still amazed me that the scar was that big and that the wood nails of that porch had torn so easily through my fire suit to cause that much damage. I can remember being at the hospital as they were frantically trying to stop the bleeding, grateful it hadn't gotten to my femoral artery to where things would be really dire. The physical therapy I had done did help some to get me moving again, but after a while, I decided I didn't want to do it anymore and just did work on my own to get better.

I got out of the shower and wrapped myself in one of the large towels Mom had in the linen closet in the bathroom. Even if she didn't know we were coming, everything about the house seemed like it was ready for guests at any moment. I looked in the mirror and could see a few days of stubble on my chin, but I decided I couldn't be bothered with shaving it off today and just left it the way it was. I didn't really care if some lawyer didn't like that I wasn't clean shaven for my appointment.

After brushing my teeth, I opened the bathroom door to go back to my room to dress. As soon as I opened the door, the steam came rushing out into the hallway. I also saw Abby and mother both standing there, waiting to get into the bathroom. Mom seemed a little more congenial than Abby, who was scowling at me.

"It's about time!" she shouted as she pushed past me and went into the bathroom, closing the door loudly.

"Gotta love girls that age," I said to Mom as I rolled my eyes. My mother was looking at me when I realized I just had a towel around me, making me feel a bit embarrassed.

"When did you get the tattoos?" she remarked to me as she saw the tattoo on my upper right arm and the one on my left shoulder.

"Oh those," I said casually. "The one here," as I pointed to my arm, "was when Abby was about year old or so." It was a jagged piece of rock with Abby's name in the center with her birthdate.

"The one on my shoulder is more recent, just a few years ago I guess. It was something all the guys in the firehouse had done. It was our firehouse shield with the 32 on it to recognize the team, something we were all proud to get and own."

"I see," Mom said, trying not to judge, but clearly judging.

"It's not a big deal Mom, really." I suddenly felt like I was a teenager again, trying to explain why I was out so late.

"You're a grown man Travis," she said to me. "You can do as you like, you know that. I just never saw the sense in tattoos. Your father had his from his time in the Army, and I never liked it."

I could remember Dad showing off the tattoo on his arm. It was something that he was always proud of, even if he rarely talked about his military time. He was in the military at a time when there wasn't much activity going on, so he never saw any action, which I think disappointed him in a way, and maybe led to why he drank so much.

"I'm going to get dressed now," I said to my mother, feeling more uncomfortable by the moment standing there in my towel. The bathroom door opened and Abby brushed past me again.

"Abby, you need to get dressed and come with me this morning," I said to her as she went towards her bedroom.

"Why? I thought I could go with Grandma this morning to the restaurant," she said, pouting.

I glanced over at my mother, hoping she would give me a look that showed some support for my side for a change. Mom finally got the hint and replied to Abby.

"I'm pretty busy there in the morning Abs," Mom told her. " I wouldn't really be able to spend much time with you down there. You're better off going with your Dad."

"I can help you out," she said hoping to sway her Grandmother with her green eyes and smile.

"I'll tell you what," Mom said to her as she put her arm around her and led her towards Abby's room. "You can come with me tomorrow and spend the whole day at the restaurant. Saturdays are the day when I can use the most help anyway. Sound good to you?" Mom looked over at me, and I nodded.

"Okay," Abby said reluctantly going along with the plan. She walked into her bedroom and shut the door to get dressed.

"Thanks, Mom," I said as I walked down the hall to my bedroom so I could get moving.

I put on a simple blue dress shirt and a pair of jeans to wear to the lawyer's office. How good did you have to look just to sign some papers? I pulled my boots on and headed down the hall and made sure to knock on Abby's door.

"Are you ready?" I shouted through the door.

"Give me just one minute Dad!" she yelled back, sounding frustrated that I would even ask.

I went downstairs to pour myself a cup of coffee before we left. Mom apparently could get ready in the blink of an eye and was already dressed to head out to the restaurant, pouring coffee into a travel mug for herself. She then handed me another travel mug she had already filled for me.

"How did you get ready so fast?" I said to her as I took a sip of coffee.

"When you do it so often it comes naturally, Travis." She said as she put the coffee pot down. "Besides, you were always painfully slow in the mornings. I had to rush you out every day, so you didn't miss the school bus."

"Well apparently my daughter takes after me now," I replied.

"She's a young girl, Travis," Mom said to me, lowering her voice a little. "You have to start making some allowances for her. She's growing up, changing, is more worried about how she looks, all that stuff."

"I don't even want to think about all that stuff yet Mom. I am far from ready to have boys crawling around looking at her."

"It's probably already happening Travis," she said as she sipped her coffee. "You just haven't seen it."

That was just one more log to add to the fire with everything else going on. Obviously, I knew Abby was growing up, I just hated to believe it was happening so fast. She was only a few months from turning thirteen, and then it was just a short while before she started high school. The thought of sending her to high school where we lived right now might be enough to get me to reconsider coming to Canon, though I knew boys that age acted crazy everywhere.

Abby appeared behind me, wearing a pair of denim shorts and a simple gray t-shirt. She had her earbuds hanging around her neck already and had her backpack with her.

"What are you bringing?" I asked her quizzically.

"It's my laptop," she said to me, clutching her bag. "I don't know how long you are going to be with this guy; I need something to pass the time."

I just shrugged and leaned down and gave my Mom a kiss on the cheek.

"I'll call you and let you know how things go," I said to her.

"Why don't you two plan to come to the restaurant for dinner tonight?" Mom said to me. "Otherwise I won't see you until tomorrow morning. By the time I get home, you two will be long asleep."

I groaned at the thought of going to the restaurant, but I knew she was going to want me there so we could eat together.

"I guess so," I conceded and saw Abby's face light up at the decision.

"Great," Mom said to me. "I will see you two tonight. I need to run; I have to stop at the dry cleaners to pick up a few things before work." She kissed Abby on her forehead as she went past her and out the door.

"Let's go get this over with," Abby said to me, tugging me to get moving out the door.

I couldn't argue with her; I wanted to get this over with too. We followed my Mom out the door and went to my car to head over to Rogers' office.

10

Travis

The ride over to Rogers' office, short as it was (what in this town isn't a short ride away?), was quiet and uneventful. Abby sat in the seat next to me, not uttering a word, as she listened to her music. I glanced over at her a few times, to see if she was even looking at the window to see what the town was like, but she showed little interest in what was going by. I tried to think of topics in my head that would be good for conversation, but I could never seem to come up with anything lately to connect with her. So we rode on for the few minutes, with the only sound the light hum of whatever song she happened to be listening to at the moment going through the air.

We arrived at Rogers' office a little after nine. I had figured since he said the office opened at nine that he would actually be there to meet us, but, as things were going for me lately, that wasn't going to happen. We were greeted by his admin, a woman by the name of Carol, who said Mr. Rogers was expected shortly. Carol was a friendly woman who looked to be in her early sixties, and she sat back down behind her desk while Abby and I waited in the less-than-comfortable vinyl-backed chairs that were in the outer office. Abby continued to fiddle with her iPod while I just looked around, hoping that we could get this over with quickly. I didn't expect that Dad had much that I would have to deal with beyond the house and whatever was in it. I did wonder about the condition of the house and whether it would be a good place for Abby and me to live. It would be nice for her to be closer to my Mom since she was the only family we had at this point. Canon, though a small town, wasn't an awful place to live. My only fear was what I was going to do with the rest of my life. The fire department wanted me to take my disability and retire. After twelve years, my pension was going to be enough to live on, but I was still too young to just sit around and, well, risk the threat of becoming like my father. I wanted something to do, but I didn't know what else I would be good at doing. I never finished beyond the one year of college, and I couldn't see myself sitting in a classroom with a bunch of teenagers listening to lectures about God knows what today. There were a lot of decisions on the horizon for me, and I wasn't sure just which way to go with any of them.

We sat around the office for a lot longer than I had wanted to. Carol kept giving us nervous glances and apologizing for having to wait so long for Mr. Rogers. She even tried calling his cell phone a few times or sending him text messages, but he never responded to any of them. Abby would give me the occasional dirty look as she sank lower and lower into the chair she was sitting in, and she finally asked Carol if there was Wi-Fi here so she could plug in her laptop and do something more entertaining. Carol led her to the small conference room off to the side so she could at least entertain herself.

Finally, after about ninety minutes of waiting and me threatening to just leave and come back another time, Irv Rogers rushed through the door. It was obvious he was having a bad morning. His gray suit was all rumpled, his tie was mostly pulled out, and what little hair he had on his head was sticking up all over the place. He rushed passed me, slammed his briefcase down on his desk in his office just beyond Carol, and then rushed back out to where Carol and I were.

"This has been an awful morning," he said to Carol as he straightened out his suit and fiddled with his tie. "My car wouldn't start at all this morning, so I called Greg down at the shop, and it took them forever to get a truck over to my house. Then they spent twenty minutes fooling around with the car trying to get it going and of course, it wouldn't. After they finally towed it to the shop, I had to wait around to talk to Greg about it and then find a ride over here. He's all the way on the other side of town. Otherwise, I would have walked."

The other side of town is about a mile from here, I thought to myself. Taking a closer look at Irv Rogers, he was clearly in no shape to walk that mile without the risk of keeling over. He was overweight, and that was being kind, and he looked to be in his fifties. His face was beet-red just from getting angry, and that was probably enough to push him too close to having some kind of cardiac event.

After he calmed down a bit while ranting at Carol, Carol was able to interrupt him long enough to let him know who I was. Irv walked over and extended his sweaty palm to me, and I reluctantly took it and gave him a brief handshake.

"It's nice to finally meet you Mr. Stone," he said to me. "Please, come in my office."

I followed him into the small office, and he closed the door behind us to give us some privacy. The office itself was very sparse, with his desk and a couple of chairs in front of it, a couple of bookcases and filing cabinets, his computer on his desk, and his law degree on the wall, along with a few pictures. Irv worked his way behind his desk and sat down with a large exhale, catching his breath. I hoped he would make it through the meeting.

"Now, let me see what I have here," as he turned on his computer to get it going and took out a folder on his desk that I assumed dealt with my father.

"Your father's will was pretty straightforward," he said to me as he looked the papers over. "I had drawn it up for him years back. He left everything to you and, well, was very particular about making sure your mother wasn't left anything, I'm afraid."

"I don't think my mother will mind," I said to Irv bluntly.

"Yes, I imagine not. That was a messy thing years back I guess, wasn't it? In any case, there's the house, which was all paid for at the time of his death. There are some things you will need to cover to get the electricity and such turned on, and there may be some taxes owed, but beyond that, it's free and clear. I'm not sure what exactly is in the house; I haven't been over there in years, but that's all yours as well. There's also a matter of what he had in his bank account and his life insurance."

"I didn't realize he had any insurance," I said to Irv, surprised my father was responsible enough to have life insurance. I also wondered why he would even bother with it. He wasn't going to leave anything to my mother, that's for sure, and I hadn't seen him in almost fifteen years.

"Oh yes, he took a policy out, well, right after he and your mother split up. He kept up with the payments all this time, so it's still active. You'll have to deal with the insurance company directly to get that all squared away, but here's the information on it."

Irv handed me some papers, and I briefly scanned them. Apparently, he had a term-life policy for $200,000. I was shocked to see that. Irv then handed me his bank account information, and that shocked me just as much. Dad had over $75,000 in the bank. I knew he had his army pension to live on for all these years, but he must have really squirreled everything away.

"How did he have this much money?" I said out loud.

"Your father didn't live on much," Rogers said to me as he leaned back in his chair. "He had few bills since the house was paid for and I think he lived a pretty quiet life for all these years."

I had lots of papers to sign to finalize things, and according to Irv, there would be more papers in the coming days as ownership of everything got transferred to me. He graciously offered to take care of it all for me, saying my father had paid for his services upfront to cover costs like this, another shocking statement to me.

He handed me the keys to the house, which included the keys to the front and back doors and the keys to the garage behind the house.

"Oh, there's one other thing," he said to me. Irv rose from his desk and lumbered over to a safe he had in the corner of the office. He got down on one knee (which was no easy feat for him, or for me to watch), pressed the buttons for the security code, and opened the safe. He took some things out and then walked back over to me, placing a small box and an envelope in front of me.

"What's this?" I said to him.

"Well, the envelope is a letter your father had written to you and left it with me to be opened upon his death. The box is, well, your father's ashes. That was another stipulation in his will."

Dad's final parting shot to me, I suppose, I thought to myself. I picked up the small box. It weighed more than I thought it would and leave it to Dad to not pay extra for an urn or anything. A plain brown box suited him just fine.

"I'll let you know if I need you for anything else," Irv said to me, extending his still sweaty hand once again. "Will you be around town for a bit?"

"Yes, I'll be here for a while," I replied, knowing I really didn't know where else I was going to go at this point. I shook Irv's hand and headed out of the office. I walked over to the conference room to corral Abby, who was typing away on her laptop when I came in.

"Let's go, kiddo," I said to her as she looked up from her keyboard. She gathered her things quickly and put them in her backpack and followed me out the door. We said a polite goodbye to Carol and walked out to my car.

"What's that?" Abby said to me as she slid into the front passenger's seat and put her seatbelt on.

I placed the box on the center console between the two of us.

"That's your grandfather," I said to her matter-of-factly, as I started the car.

"That's gross Dad," she said as she tried to inch away from the box.

"It's his ashes; Don't worry, he won't jump out and grab you."

I started up the car and headed over to Collins Drive where the house was. It was already almost noon, and it had taken much longer than I thought it would to get this stuff done.

"Where are we going?" Abby said to me, taking an interest in what was going on for the first time in a long time.

"Over to his house," I said to her as I tried to remember exactly where Collins Drive was. I navigated my way through the side streets so we could get over to the house and see what was there.

"Why are we going there?" Abby asked, creeped out by what we might find there.

"Well, because it's our house now I guess," I said to her as we got closer to where the house was.

"No way!" she said with some excitement. "We have a house? Does that mean we are going to live here?" This was as happy and excited as I had seen her in a long time.

"I'm not sure yet, honey," I said to her, trying to calm her down, so she didn't get her hopes up too high. "I have to see what the house is like, what we need to do to it, and so on. There's a lot of details we would still have to work out before we decide on something like that."

I pulled into the driveway next to the house and drove back towards the garage. I parked the car and Abby and I both got out warily, looking at the back of the house. The house needed a new paint job for sure, and the lawn was well overgrown in the back and the front. We got up to the front gate and unlatched it letting ourselves in. Abby reached down and plucked something out of the grass and held it in her hands. It was a long blue ribbon, like what someone might use to tie their hair. She held it, studying it as we walked slowly up the rickety front steps towards the door of the house. We were both a little nervous about what we might find inside.

11

Sophie

The whole ride over to the school from the Homestead was just like a blur to me. I barely remember concentrating on the road and thinking more about Travis and how things were now. Before I knew it, I was parking my car in the customary spot in the parking lot right next to Mary's. I was glad she was actually here and hopped out of my car and found myself pratically running through the front doors and towards her classroom, which was one door down from mine. The hallways were empty and quiet, just as they always are this time of year, and I could hear my sneakers squeaking on the polished floor as I ran, making a loud squeak as I stopped short in front of her classroom. I threw the door open, feeling a little out of breath.

Mary looked up from her paperwork on her desk with a surprised look. "What are you doing? Is everything okay?"

She surely wasn't used to seeing me this excited. I grabbed a chair from one of the desks nearby and sat down right next to her. I reached over and grabbed her hands, more to get mine to stop trembling from excitement than anything else.

"He's here," I said to her as I couldn't contain my smile any longer.

"Who? Kenny? What did he ask you to this time?" she said as she turned her face back down to her paperwork.

"No, not Kenny," I said to her, pulling the papers away from her so she could look at me. "Travis. Travis is in Canon."

"THE Travis?" Mary said with wonder. Now I had her attention.

"Remember the red-headed girl we saw last night at the Homestead with Maggie?" I said to her, trying to control myself a little bit.

"Sure, how could you miss her? No one in this town has red hair like that."

"That's Travis' daughter," I said to her. "I saw her eyes last night, and she has his eyes. I knew they were related somehow. I spent all night thinking about it, so I went to see Maggie at lunchtime this afternoon and asked her. She confirmed it; she's his daughter."

"And how is this good news for you?" she asked, turning to face me now, curious where I was going.

"I didn't think it would be either, but Maggie told me he's not married. He's never been married. The girl – Abby is her name – the girl's mother left them when she was a baby. He's raised her himself. He's still single."

"And he's here in Canon? Are you sure he's going to be here for a while?" Mary said to me. This put a pinhole in my balloon.

"Well, no I don't know that for certain," I said to her as I got up from the chair and started pacing a bit. "But if Travis is here there's a chance we could run into each other."

"Do you hear yourself, Sophie?" Mary said to me as she stood up in front of me to stop me from pacing. "There's a chance we could run into each other? You've been hung up on this guy for how long? Fourteen or fifteen years? I don't want to rain on your parade, I really don't, but if he's been single this long, why hasn't he ever come back here to Canon? Or tried to find you? People aren't that hard to track down nowadays you know. Facebook, the Internet, all that stuff – I do plenty of cyberstalking of old boyfriends; it's pretty easy to do."

Mary made some good points that stopped me in my tracks. I couldn't come up with an immediate reason as to why he never tried to find me after all these years. It could be that he lost interest, gave up hope, gave up on me, but I didn't want to believe it.

"Okay, you make a good point," I said to her. "But that doesn't matter. The fact is that Travis is here now, for whatever reason, even if it isn't to find out about me. We could still run into each other, see each other, and maybe…"

"If you want to see him, Sophie, let's just make it happen. Why does it have to be by accident? I know Canon is a small town, but suppose he was leaving today? Your chance might already be gone. Let's go to the Homestead again tonight for dinner. It's his mother's place. I think the odds are good that he would be there, especially if his daughter were there. Then you can guarantee you see him and we'll see what happens."

I knew Mary was right. I couldn't just hope that he would magically run into me on the street somehow, sparks would fly, and he would tell me he still loves me after all these years. This wasn't a romance story after all; it was real life.

"You're right Mary," I said to her nervously. "We'll go back to the Homestead tonight for dinner and see if he is there. If he is, we'll see what happens." I tried to sound as grown up about it as I could, but inside I felt like I was that eighteen-year-old girl again.

"Fair enough," Mary said to me. "We'll head over there around five. That should get us there before the Friday crowd for dinner so we can get a table and scope things out. Until then, I really do have work to do," she glanced down to the papers on her desk then back up to me. "Do you think you can contain yourself until five?" she said, smiling at me. She could see me practically jumping up and down at the prospect of what could happen tonight.

"I'll try," I told her as I walked towards the door, figuring I would go to my classroom and pretend to do work for a few hours until we could leave. The excitement I felt in my body had replaced that anxious knot that was in my stomach just a little while ago. I walked into my classroom, sat down at my desk, and tried to concentrate on lesson plans, class rosters and the like. This was not going to be an easy few hours.

12

Travis

Based on the worn condition outside the house, I was more than a little worried about what I would find inside the house. I warily unlocked the front door, and Abby and I stepped inside. What we saw made both of us stare in wonder.

"This place looks immaculate," Abby said as she slowly walked around the living room as we got inside.

I was in complete shock. It looked as if the place was in pristine condition, almost as if it had just been cleaned up. I know I hadn't seen my father in years, but he was never the kind of guy to go crazy with housecleaning. He usually just left that to my mother, saying it was "woman's work" as he put himself in his chair and sat down to have a beer and watch TV. I had expected to find dust and dirt, and probably trash strewn all over, but everything was in its place, neat and tidy, and there was no dust at all, which seemed almost impossible. Irv Rogers had said he hadn't been out here, so no one had been in the house since Dad died, yet it looked sparkling.

Abby wandered around the house into the kitchen and then back out to the living room.

"The kitchen is perfect," she said to me. "There's not even anything in the fridge except a few bottles of beer." Now that sounded like Dad, but you would expect some spoiled food if no one had been in here in a month or more.

I kept looking around the living room, seeing it was pretty sparse for furniture. Dad's customary leather recliner was right where I would have expected it to be, near the front window so he could get some light without having to turn the lights on. There were a sofa and coffee table, and a small bureau that had his record player on it with a few records next to it. I looked through the two drawers in the bureau but found little there outside of some old mail and paperwork.

I decided to go upstairs and have a look around there. If anything, maybe I would find something in Dad's bedroom. The stairs creaked lightly as I made my way up the steps. I looked down the short hall at the top of the stairs. Dad's bedroom was down the end of the hall to the right, and then there was a bathroom, a closet, and another bedroom at the end on the left. I decided to start in his bedroom to get a look around.

The bed looked freshly made, and the bedroom was clean as well. Just as I expected, there wasn't much in the bedroom. Dad had his dresser, a night table, and an old wooden chair in there, and that was it. I looked through the dresser, finding nothing but clothing inside. On top of the tall, oak dresser was some cologne, and a few trinkets Dad must have picked up along the way, but nothing that would tell me anything about him.

The nightstand offered a little more, with some bills with a rubber band around them, but nothing out of the ordinary. There was an extra pair of reading glasses on the nightstand and a pen and a pad there next to the phone.

I opened the accordion door to the closet and saw Dad's suits and shirts hanging there. Nothing looked new, which was keeping with Dad's style. I rarely remember him wearing a suit unless he was going to a funeral. A few pairs of shoes were at the bottom of the closet, but nothing else. There was one small box on the shelf in the closet, and it looked to be a black security box. I figured if anything it might have something else in it. I pulled the box down, and it looked as if the lock was broken on it. When I opened the box, I saw a couple of medals Dad got while in the Army. He also had one of my old wrestling medals in the box as well. I had no idea he had kept it, let alone ever even came to one of my matches in high school. The box also held some basic papers, like the deed to the house, his discharge papers, social security card, birth certificate and nothing else.

I placed the box on the bed and went down the hall, opening the closet door as I passed it. Nothing but towels and bathroom supplies were in there, and an old white robe was hanging on the back of the door. I popped into the other bedroom at the end of the hall. I remembered the room vaguely from the few times I stayed with Dad when I was seventeen, and expected it to be the same, but to my surprise, the room looked different. It was clean as well and seemed brighter than I had remembered it. It had a full-size bed in the room and a small dresser and nightstand, with a small closet opposite where the bed was in the room. There were no items in the dresser, nightstand or closet to speak of, which seemed odd to me. As I looked around the room, I noticed the light purple color of the paint on the walls. The best I could remember, the walls were always plain white in here. This paint looked like it was fairly new, with not a mark on it.

Abby came up behind into the room to look around.

"Is this going to be my room?" she said with some excitement as she fell back onto the bed.

"I guess it would be if we stayed here," I told her, unable to figure anything else out.

"Awesome!" she said as she looked around. I could see her brain working behind those green eyes as she figured out how she would decorate the room to make it her own. I smiled as I watched her, feeling glad that she seemed happy with something for a change.

"I'm going to go check out the garage," I said to her as I walked out of the room. "You coming with me?"

"I think I am going to hang out here for a bit," she said to me as she looked around the room and out the window, which looked out onto the small backyard.

"Okay, be careful," I said to her.

"Really, Dad?" she said to me, bringing back the irked preteen tone to her voice. "What is going to happen?"

"Nevermind," I mumbled as I walked out of the room. I went down the stairs and towards the kitchen, where there was a door leading out to the back porch and the back of the house where the garage was. I unlocked the back door and stepped out onto the porch. The porch needed a new paint job, and some of the boards seemed warped, worn or damaged. Dad obviously cared more about the inside of the house than the outside.

I went down the two steps of the back porch, feeling the last step crack a bit under my weight as I moved, making me stumble a bit out into the overgrown grass in the backyard.

I heard the window open above me and looked up to see Abby sticking her head out the window.

"Be careful Dad," she said with a smile.

I smiled back at her and nodded at her smart-aleck statement. I walked through the taller grass over to the garage. The white paint on the garage, much like the paint on the house, was chipped and showed a lot of wear. The garage wasn't very large, and the roll gate was locked from the inside. I used the key Rogers had given me to unlock the door to the garage and walked in.

The air inside was very stale, indicating no one had been in here for a while. There was plenty of dust to be found here, with a lot of it covering the small counters where Dad had his tools lined up. The tools looked like they didn't get much use, and there was also a small lawn mower tucked into the corner with some other lawn tools. To my surprise, there was also a vehicle under a blue tarp.

For as long as I could remember, Dad rarely drove. I give him credit for that much since he liked to drink and never took the chance of getting behind the wheel. He always walked to where he would drink, usually at The Rail Station, the bar in town located right near the train station here, since Mom wouldn't let him drink at the Homestead. It was less than a half mile from my mother's house, and somehow he always made it back, no matter how much he had to drink that night.

I pulled the tarp back to get a look at what was underneath and saw that it was a red pickup truck. The truck looked pretty new and based on a quick look at the registration sticker on the window I could see it was just a year old at most. Rogers hadn't given me a key to any vehicles, so apparently, he didn't know about it. I looked at the counters to see if I could find the keys but I didn't see them anywhere. I checked the few drawers there as well without any luck, and nothing seemed to be hanging on the walls anywhere.

I then remembered the old trick Mom did with stashing the key to the house in the broken shingle. I checked the wheel wells of the car and there, in the front driver's side well, was a small case. I pulled the case out, and there was the key, on a fob with an automatic door opener. I pressed it, half-expecting it not to work, and heard the familiar sound of the locks shifting to open.

I climbed into the front seat of the truck and sat there, not knowing what to do. The inside of the cab still smelled brand new, and a quick glance at the odometer showed there were only 113 miles on the truck, meaning Dad barely used the truck at all. I looked inside the glove compartment and found the insurance and registration for the car, confirming that the car was only a few months old. After a quick look around inside the cab, I opened the center console, not expecting to find anything in there. There was nothing but a pair of sunglasses.

I flipped down the sun visor on the driver's side and found the extra car key and fob tucked in there, along with a picture. It was odd that Dad didn't have any other pictures anywhere in the house now that I thought about it. I flipped the picture over, and there was Dad, standing in front of a picnic table, with his arm around a woman who looked to be about my age on one side of him, and then a young girl on the other side of him. There was no indication or markings on the photo, and looking closer it looked like the picture was taken at Wilson Park, the one park located in town that had some picnic areas and play areas for kids.

I didn't recognize the woman or child. The woman was just about Dad's height, with short brown hair and dark eyes. She was beaming proudly in the picture, and surprisingly, Dad was smiling just as wide, something I rarely saw him do. The girl on the other side of him looked to be about twelve or thirteen and had the same eyes and hair as the woman, making me assume it was mother and daughter.

Why would Dad keep this picture in here? I asked myself, sitting back in the truck. I studied the picture a little bit more trying to figure it all out. Could it be a girlfriend? Dad was a charmer for sure, even when I was younger, it was clear about that, and he loved to flirt. It was a bit of a mystery.

I took the picture and the keys to the truck and went out of the garage, locking the door behind me. I walked back up the steps to the back porch and went into the kitchen. I sat down at the kitchen table, an unimpressive, old Formica table that looked like it came from a flea market or garage sale. The chairs matched it, and the one I sat in seemed unsteady. I studied the picture a little longer, trying to figure it out, but nothing was coming to me.

It was then I remembered the letter Rogers gave me. I took the envelope I had folded in half out of jeans' pocket and held it in front of me. I hesitated a little before opening it, a little afraid of what I might find in there. I didn't really know what to expect from it. I tore open one end of the envelope, blew into it, and slid the letter out. I unfolded the letter and saw that it was handwritten by my Dad. Dad was never much of one for computers, so that wasn't much of a surprise. I began to read the short letter.

Travis,

I know I wasn't always the best person to be around, for you or your mother. Your mother and I had our problems, but just know none of that had anything to do with you. It wasn't until after I was out of the house that I learned more about myself and how I had treated you and your mother. I wish I could take back some of what I had done and said over the years, and I am sorry we never got the chance to get back together again so we could actually get to know each other, and so that I could get to know my granddaughter.

My one piece of advice to you is this – don't let your life have any regrets to it like mine did. They will eat you up inside. Take advantage of the opportunities that come along to make yourself and your daughter happy. That's what is most important in life.

No matter what I may have done or said over the years, know that I was always proud of you. I'm just sorry I never got to tell you in person. Be a better man to your family than I was to mine.

Dad

I re-read the letter several times, and I could feel myself choke up a bit after each read. My father never gave much of an indication that he cared what I was doing or how I lived my life, but I guess I had read him wrong. Something obviously changed for him over the years, and now I was sorry I never got the chance to find out what it was.

I stood up out of the chair and walked back out into the living room. Abby was sitting on the couch looking at her phone. I went over and sat down next to her, putting my arm around her so I could pull her closer to me. I expected her to resist a little, much as she had for the last few months, but instead, I think she could sense what I was feeling and came close to me, putting her head on my shoulder.

"What's that?" she asked as she saw what I was holding in my hand.

"It's the letter from my father," I said to her, placing it back in my pocket.

"What's the picture?" she said to me. I held the picture out for her to see.

"I'm not really sure," I told Abby. "It's your grandfather with a woman and girl. I don't know who they are."

Abby took the picture in her right hand and studied it. I realized then that she had never seen a picture of Dad when he was older. I had some pictures of me from when I was a kid, but he was in very few of them. Since she never got to see much of him, it was natural that she had some interest. She looked closely at the picture and then handed it back to me.

"He had your smile," she said to me quietly.

I hugged her tightly with my left arm that was around her and kissed her on top of her head.

"Yeah, I guess we had the same smile," recognizing it for the first time myself.

"What have you been up to?" I asked, to see what she had been doing while I was exploring.

"Nothing much, just messing with my phone. Oh, I never showed you the picture I got of Grandma and me last night at the restaurant." Abby sat up and worked her fingers magically over her phone to pull up the picture. She handed me the phone so I could see it.

There was Abby, smiling with her arm around my Mom, who was grinning from ear to ear. It was a nice picture of the two of them. As I went to hand the phone back to Abby. I stopped abruptly to take a closer look at the picture. I pulled the phone closer to my face so I could get a better look.

There in the background, behind Abby and my mother, was someone looking into the camera as well. The blonde hair and face were unforgettable for me. It was Sophie, without a doubt.

"Dad, are you okay?" Abby said to me as she sat up.

I stood up from the couch and handed the phone back to her.

"We need to get over to the restaurant. Now."

13

Travis

After Abby and I got in the car, my mind was still pretty distracted. I was torn between who it was that my father had this other life with and the notion that Sophie was here in Canon. I hadn't seen Sophie since the end of that summer after our freshman year at college. I had decided at that point that I didn't want to go back to college, that it had little to offer me, and I was ready to move on with my life. I had already signed up to take the fireman's exam and was ready to do that, and I was hoping Sophie was ready to start a life with me, away from college, away from Canon.

Unfortunately, she didn't see it the same way. To her, school was important, and it was her goal to get her education, become a teacher, and make a difference that way. She never planned on coming back to Canon, at least when we had talked about life after college. She had ambitions of becoming a teacher at a school somewhere that needed a lot of help, like an inner city. I tried to plead with her that she could still do that and go with me to wherever we would end up, but she didn't seem ready to give up the life she had at school, or in Canon, even though there wasn't much keeping her here. Like me, she was an only child and basically grew up with just a mother in her life. Her father had left when we were in grade school together, and it hit her pretty hard. She was attached to her mother, and even through high school she didn't go out much. We never moved in the same circles, but I sure noticed her, even if it was from afar.

She has always had that something special about her. It was more than just the way she looked. Sophie was always very pretty, and her blue eyes could certainly catch attention, but to me, it was her radiant smile and the sweet way that she seemed to approach life. She was nice to everyone, even if people weren't nice to her, because that's just the way she was. I never was able to work up the courage to ask her out in high school because I always felt she was smarter than me and could do better. When I got to college that freshman year and saw her at orientation, it was like we were drawn to each other right away.

There we were, two kids away from home for the first time, and we found someone from that little hole-in-the-wall town we were from. We clung to each other for weeks after that until we started to get settled in and meet people. By then, I was completely in love with her but still couldn't tell her that. It was only after we went to a party together after a football game, and I had way too much to drink and was sitting outside with her, that I told her how I felt about her. She said she had feelings for me as well, and that was the night of our first kiss.

After that we were inseparable. I walked Sophie to different classes each day, we had meals together, went out on dates and to parties, and spent as much time together as possible. I loved being with her and wanted to be as close to her as possible, but she made it clear to me almost from the start that she was virgin and planned to stay that way for now. I respected her decision, as frustrating as it could be at times. Some of our make-out sessions would go on for a long time, and we would end up in various states of undress, but it never went any further than that.

By the time the spring semester had ended, and we came home together, I was deeply in love with her. She came over to my mother's house for meals and to hang out, or we hung out at the restaurant. I worked there over the summer while she worked at Simmons, the local department store, in the women's department. She would come over to the restaurant after her shift and sit with me or help me clean up after closing. Then we would stay up watching movies, talking on the porch, or making out in my room.

We didn't spend much time at her house since her mother didn't really approve of her having a boyfriend. She wanted Sophie to commit herself to school and not get distracted, and her mother made it very clear to me that Sophie had goals and ideas that were to be honored. It wasn't until the end of summer approached, and it was almost time to go back to school, that I sprang my plan on her. The notion intrigued her, of us living together somewhere while I became a fireman, but that initial intrigue was gone by the next day. Sophie told me she needed to go back to school and begged me to go with her. I told her I couldn't give up on my dream any more than she could give up on hers. We argued, there were tears, and when everything was said, she hugged me goodnight. The next day when I went to her mother's house to see her, Mrs. Ingram told me she had left early to go back to school. That was the last time I saw her.

That was fourteen years ago, and now here she was, in my mother's restaurant, in the same picture as my daughter. Was she just visiting her own mother in town? I wasn't even sure if Mrs. Ingram was still living in Canon. Maybe she was passing through and stopped in to see friends. Or maybe she lived here now. It seemed like more than my brain could take at the moment.

The car seemed to drive itself over to the Homestead. Since it was only nearly 4 PM, there wasn't much going on in there. Lunch was long over, and dinner had yet to start. I parked in the parking lot and Abby, and I hopped out. Abby raced to the front door and through, excited to go see her grandmother and let her know about the house. I, on the other hand, had other things I needed to find out about.

When I got through the front door, I saw Abby standing over at the bar talking to Mom. I strode over, feeling a mix of anger, confusion, and excitement. Abby was going a mile a minute about the house and how great it was while Mom was just nodding along. I stood behind Abby and waited for her to finish rambling on. When she finally paused, Mom looked up at me and saw I had a serious look on my face.

"Hey Abs, why don't you go to the kitchen and see if Henry needs any help with some prep work," she said to Abby calmly.

Abby looked at me, and that back at my mother, and saw we needed to talk.

"Sure Grandma," she said cautiously and walked over through the swinging doors into the kitchen. Mom got back behind the bar and was straightening things up.

"What's wrong, Travis?" she said to me as she put glassware away. "You have that look on your face you used to get when you were young, and something was troubling you. Everything alright at the house? Abby seemed to think so."

I sat on one of the stools and talked as Mom kept cleaning.

"The house was fine. The outside needs some work, but the inside was, well, perfect. It looked like the maids had just come through and cleaned the whole thing."

Mom turned and faced me with a stunned look.

"Really? Your father's house? That man never cleaned a damn thing when he lived with us."

"I remember. It was pretty puzzling. The place was spotless. No food in the fridge, the beds were made, no dust, the floor was clean. It was like someone was expecting Dad to come home at any minute."

Mom poured me a beer from the tap and passed it over to me. I took a long sip of the cold red ale she gave me. It felt great going down after a long day.

"There were some other puzzling things too," I told her. "Did you know Dad had an insurance policy? And a ton of money in the bank?" I explained what Irv Rogers had told me and Mom couldn't believe it.

"That cheap weasel," she said as she reached over, grabbed a shot glass, and poured herself a shot of whiskey and downed it. "All this time he could have afforded to live comfortably on his own. I guess he got the last laugh."

I then took the letter that Dad had written me and passed it over to her so she could read it. She slipped her reading glasses on and read the letter a few times. She looked over at me and could see I was feeling guilty.

"Travis," she said as she took my hand, "don't feel guilty about the way things played out. Your father chose his path in life, and you chose yours. He could have reached out to you at any time, but he didn't. Goodness knows he had his faults – lots of them – but deep down I know he loved you and was proud of you. He was just too stubborn to ever say it to you."

"Well I was too stubborn to ever come and see him," I said as I took another long sip of beer.

"You had to live your life, Travis. For you and for Abby. He didn't know you were taking care of her on your own. Hell, we lived in the same small town together for years, and I never ran into him more than once or twice from the time you left until the day he died. He never said one word to me either. He'd tip that ratty old hat he always wore to me and just walk on by."

I had forgotten about the ratty old hat. Dad always wore this tweed cap around town. It always looked out of place on him, but he loved it. It had lasted forever, but now that Mom mentioned it, I hadn't seen it in the house. It was then I remembered the picture.

"I also found this in the truck he had in the garage," I said to her as I handed her the picture.

"Your father had a truck?" she said loudly, causing the waitresses setting the tables for dinner to turn around and take a look at her. "Why did he have a truck?" she asked me. "He never drove anywhere."

Mom took a close look at the picture.

"That's Emma Winters," she said to me without batting an eye.

"Who is that? " I asked her. She continued to study the picture a bit longer before she looked up at me and handed it back to me.

"That's the waitress who worked here that night…" she paused then restarted, "It's who I caught your father fooling around with in the back room," she said abruptly.

"Wasn't she about my age?" I asked her.

"She was little older than you," she said to me as she took the picture and looked at it again. "She was nineteen when she was working here. Out of high school, didn't go to college and wanted a full-time job. She was a very pretty girl, smart, funny and a great waitress. I really liked her. Apparently, your father did too. I had no idea he kept seeing her. I've seen her around town, but not much. I think she was working a few towns over now, in Sterling. This looks like it was taken just a few months ago."

"Do you think," I hesitated a bit before finishing the thought. "Do you think the girl was Dad's?"

Mom looked hard at the picture again. "I guess she could be," she said to me. "She looks about Abby's age. That would mean it was about two years after you left here, so your father was about forty. It sure could be his daughter. There is a bit of a resemblance in the face."

Now I had even more to consider. Dad led this secret life, and I had a half-sister out there somewhere the same age as my daughter. I finished my beer and rubbed my forehead with my hand.

"This is a lot for you to take in one day, I know Travis," Mom said to me calmly.

"Oh, wait, there's more," I said to her.

"What else could there be?" she said throwing her arms up in the air. "It's not enough to drop all this, but on top of your stuff I have had two of my bartenders up and quit today. Seems as though they ran off with each other last night and I am left high and dry for a bartender on a Friday night."

"Can I finish before we get to your bartender soap opera?" I said, cutting her off.

"Go ahead," Mom said as she leaned herself against the back of the bar.

"Abby showed me a picture she took with you last night here at the restaurant," I said to her.

"Yes, one of the waitresses took it for us with her phone. What about it?"

"She showed it to me today. I saw Sophie sitting behind you in the picture. Is she in town?"

Mom smiled at me and leaned forward. "As a matter of fact she is," she said to me coyly.

"Is she just visiting someone? Her mother maybe?" I was sitting there waiting with anticipation. Mom came around from behind the bar and stood next to me as I sat on the stool.

"Ruth Ingram moved out of Canon years ago," she said to me. "No, she isn't visiting anyone. Sophie is the eighth-grade English teacher here. She has been for years."

I was stunned. "And you never bothered to share this information with me before?"

"You could have come to town anytime you wanted to Travis and found out for yourself. You're the one that stayed away. You never asked me about her, so I figured you weren't interested."

I didn't know what to say next.

"Is she… is she seeing anyone?" I said, sounding like I was back in high school now.

"Sophie? Now let me think," she said as she brought her right hand up to her chin, stroking it like she was studying a painting to figure out what it meant. "Pretty girl like that, you'd have to think she was seeing someone, wouldn't you?" I knew she was just messing with me at this point.

"Can you just answer me, please?" I begged her.

"Honestly, I don't see her that much. But when I do see her, she is never with a man." Mom wiped the bar a bit with her dishrag.

My mind was racing again with all the information it was processing. Dad, Emma Winters, this girl, the house, what to do with Abby, my life and career, and now, Sophie. I wasn't sure I could take much more.

"Now that I have answered your questions," Mom mentioned, " Perhaps you can help me out with something."

"Sure Mom," I told her as I stood up from the bar stool.

"I need a bartender for tonight," she said as she handed me an apron and the dishrag.

"Mom, you don't want me behind the bar," I said, handing the items back to her.

"Why not?" she said to me. "You used to bartend before you got certified as a fireman. Even then you always bartended their parties and fundraisers. You could do it with your eyes closed. Besides," she said with a smile, "you owe me at least this one."

It was hard to argue with that, but I was still reluctant to do it. Mom could see the resistance on my face.

"You never know," she said to me in a sing-song voice as she started to walk towards the kitchen. "Sophie may come back in tonight," she turned to face me as she bumped the swinging door to the kitchen open with her backside.

I put the apron on and went to the bar to familiarize myself with the setup, hoping it would be a good night.

14

Sophie

Five o'clock never took so long to arrive for anyone. There were times when I looked at the clock in my classroom, and I could swear the time was standing still or moving backward. Every ten minutes felt like an hour as I tried to do whatever I could to occupy my mind. I must have straightened the bookcase in my room twice, I put up new posters, restocked my supplies, and even clapped the erasers even though they hadn't been used for months. Finally, when it was about ten minutes to five, and I couldn't take the waiting anymore, I packed up my belongings calmly, closed the classroom door and practically leaped into Mary's classroom.

She was still sitting at her desk working on her lesson plans. I stood in the doorway and tapped my foot on the floor repeatedly, so it echoed up and down the empty halls. She took a sly glance over at me and placed her pen down on her desk. She slowly closed her laptop, stretched and yawned for a minute, and stacked and re-stacked at her papers until I groaned in frustration. She broke out into a big grin.

"Okay, let's go," she said as she rose from her desk chair.

I was giddy with excitement. We made our way down the hallway quickly, but as soon as we got close to the main office window, we slowed down and moved quietly passed. We didn't want to arouse any attention from Kenny, who was surely still in the office passing the time shredding papers or sharpening pencils. I crept passed the window and spied him organizing something near the main desk, with his back to the window. Once I was passed, I waved Mary on to come towards me. She tore down the hall to get beyond the window as fast as possible. We then ran like schoolgirls, holding hands down the hallway, until we were outside.

Mary started to climb into her car and said to me, "Why don't you ride with me? We can leave your car here."

"What for?" I asked her, innocently.

Mary sighed at me. "Suppose Travis is there, you hit it off, and you end up going home together in his car. You don't need a car there."

I blushed at the thought of that. "That's... that's not likely to happen," I said to her, trying not to feel too embarrassed.

"Of course not," Mary said, rolling her eyes at me. "You've only been waiting for the guy for fourteen years. How silly of me. Okay, suppose you want to have a drink or two because you're so nervous about meeting him. Sound more plausible to you, Ms. Ingram?"

As much as I didn't drink, tonight might be a night where I needed some liquid courage to get through. I nodded at Mary and climbed into the passenger seat of her car.

In reality, we could have just walked to the Homestead if we wanted to from the school since nothing was too far to walk in Canon. Mary tore out of the parking lot and down the road as I held onto the dashboard.

"Try to get me there in one piece please," I begged her as she took the right turn towards the restaurant rather sharply.

Mary shot me a look and smiled, and then slowed down to a crawl as we got closer to the restaurant, moving at a snail's pace as she taunted me. When we arrived at the restaurant, she pulled into the parking lot and parked her car near the entrance. Mary sat and looked at me as she turned the car off.

"What?" I said to her, feeling self-conscious. I checked myself in the tiny mirror to see how I looked.

"You look fine, Sophie, don't worry about it. I just hope he is in there. I want to see you happy."

Mary leaned over and gave me a hug, squeezing me tight.

"Thanks, Mary," I said softly to her.

"Now let's go get that man for you," she said, clapping her hands.

We both got out of the car, and we headed for the front door. Mary held the door open for me so I could enter first. I walked in and saw that there wasn't much of a crowd in the place just yet, which was perfect for us. Mary joined me at the hostess podium, and within a moment, Maggie was greeting us.

"Well hello ladies," she said with a big smile. "Twice in one day, Sophie? This is an occasion," she said to me with a wink.

"You know how we love the food here, Maggie," Mary said to her, elbowing me lightly.

"Glad to hear it, Mary," Maggie said as she grabbed two menus. She led us over to a table in the far corner so we could get a clear look at the rest of the dining room.

"This table okay?" she asked us.

"Perfect," I told her as I smiled back at her.

"You ladies enjoy your dinner," Maggie said as she walked back towards the front of the restaurant.

There were just a couple of other tables taken so far tonight, but it wouldn't be long before the place was filled on a Friday night. There were already a few people seated at the bar as well, enjoying their Friday evening, let's-start-the-weekend-early drinks.

I tried to occupy my mind by looking at the menu, though I doubted anything on it was different from yesterday, or from when I had seen it this afternoon. I was actually starting to feel more nervous as the seconds ticked on, wondering if Travis would be here at all this evening.

A moment later, Patty was standing there in front of us to wait on us again.

"Hey, Ms. Ingram, Ms. Connors. I'm surprised to see you two here again tonight." Patty smiled at us and held up her pad. "Can I get you something to drink?"

"Cosmo me, Patty," Mary said proudly.

"You got it, Ms. Connors," Patty replied with a giggle. "Lemonade for you, Ms. Ingram?"

"I'll have... a glass of red wine, please," I said to her. Mary beamed at me and nodded in agreement.

"Really?" Patty said, sounding genuinely surprised. I just glanced up her and nodded. "Okay, I'll put them right in for you."

Patty walked away, and I glanced around the restaurant again, hoping to catch a glimpse of him coming in. So far, I didn't see any sign of him or his daughter, and I was starting to get nervous that maybe they weren't going to show. A few more tables had been filled in just a few minutes that had passed.

Patty was back pretty quickly with our drinks. She placed the drinks down and asked if we were ready to order. Mary ordered her hamburger and fries, and I found myself ordering a Cobb salad.

Patty took the order and went off to the kitchen to put it in for us.

"Since when do you eat Cobb salad?" Mary asked me.

"I like Cobb salad," I said to her defending my new favorite meal. "it has some great stuff in it."

"Whatever you want Sophie," Mary said to me. She raised her glass to me. "Here's to a promising evening," she said to me.

I raised my red wine glass to her as we clinked the glasses. Mary took a sip of her Cosmo while I downed half of my red wine.

"Whoa, easy there Sophie," she said to me. "You haven't had a drink in a while; you don't want yourself getting soused before he even walks through the door."

I could feel the warmth down my throat and spreading to my toes already.

"I'm too nervous Mary," I said to her as I took another gulp of wine. "What if he doesn't show? Worse, what if he does and doesn't remember me? Or even want to see me or talk to me? This is going to be a disaster." Before I knew it, my wine glass was empty.

"Relax Sophie," Mary said to me. "Everything is going to be fine. Just play it as it comes, without expectations."

As I sat nervously fiddling with my fork, Maggie walked over to the table. Standing next to her was the beautiful red-haired girl with the green eyes. She stood nearly as tall as Maggie, had a big smile on her face, and wore a white blouse and black slacks, with a black apron around her. She was holding a small basket of dinner rolls in front of her.

"Ladies, this is Abby, my granddaughter," she said introducing her to us. "She's working here tonight bussing tables. Abby, this is Ms. Connors and Ms. Ingram. They are both teachers at the middle school here."

"Nice to meet you both," Abby said politely as she gently placed the basket of bread on the table.

"Nice to meet you, Abby," Mary chimed in as I stared at Abby in awkward silence. I wanted to say something to her, but nothing seemed to be coming out of my mouth.

Maggie could see I was a little taken aback. "Abby, Ms. Ingram is an old friend of your dad's," she said.

"Oh yeah?" Abby said with interest as she turned her attention to me. "I haven't met many people that knew Dad when he was younger, other than Grandma," she said with a small smile. "So what was he like when he was my age?"

"Well," I managed to croak out. "We weren't very good friends until we got older," I said to her, feeling my face redden. "We did know each other when we were younger, but we didn't hang out much. I do remember that your Dad was always friendly and nice to me though."

"Too bad," she said to me. "I was hoping for some dirt on him," she said with a bigger grin. I laughed out loud, feeling a little better.

"Okay Abby, back to work," Maggie said to her, hustling her back towards the kitchen.

"Nice to meet you both!" Abby shouted as she moved away.

"Well at least you know he's still around if his daughter is still here," Mary said to me, snapping me out of my haze.

"That's true," I replied. "But I think that makes me feel more nervous because it means Travis is more likely to show up here."

Patty appeared at our table once again. "Would you ladies like some refills?" she asked us.

"Yes, please" I whispered as I shakily held up my empty glass.

"One more for me to Patty," Mary said to her, handing her the Cosmo glass.

Patty walked away from us towards the bar. I could see the place had filled up quite a bit by now, and there were even people waiting around at the front for tables. The bar was filled as well, making it harder to make out faces of who was here. Would I even recognize Travis if I saw him now? I had no idea what he looked like now, or if he looked the same. I kept looking around the room and then shooting frantic looks back to Mary.

"You need to relax Sophie," Mary said to me.

Just then a tall figure appeared next to our table, casting a shadow over the table itself.

"Patty was busy, so she asked me to bring the drinks over," the voice said as I saw the hand place the Cosmo down in front of Mary. I looked up as I saw the glass of red wine coming towards me. I mindlessly took it in my hand as I was scanning the room. As I tried to pull the glass away, I felt some resistance from the hand holding it and looked up.

"Hello, Sophie," he said to me.

I could see those green eyes and instantly knew it was Travis. I slowly drew my hand back, trying not to spill the red wine as I put the glass down on the table. He was taller than I remembered and seemed more muscular as well as he stood with his broad shoulders. He was wearing a blue dress shirt and blue jeans, and his brown hair was shorter now than I recall it being in years past, but there was no doubt it was him. He smiled down at me, waiting for some sort of response from me.

I was stumbling for words, too shocked that he was really here, in front of me. I then felt Mary kick me underneath the table to jolt me back to reality.

"Hello... hello Travis," I said to him very quietly. I brushed the hair out of my face, wishing I had looked different somehow right now. "It's been a long time."

He stood tall next to our table and smiled at me again.

"It has. Way too long of a time," Travis said.

I could feel his eyes on me, looking up and down. I tried not to look right at him, feeling like I wouldn't be able to handle it, to be strong like I should. Just having him next to me was making me feel weak. I wanted to just stand up and let him take me in his arms, and it was taking all I could to stop making a fool of myself. There was an awkward silence for a moment before Mary could see what was happening and intervened.

"Hi, I'm Mary Connors," she said to Travis, sticking her hand out to break the spell between Travis and myself.

"Hello Mary," Travis said politely as he shook her hand gently but firmly. I looked over at Mary and could see her making eyes at him, making me feel a tinge of jealousy right away.

"I've heard a lot about you Travis," Mary said with a smile as she looked at me now. I knew I was blushing deeply now, feeling embarrassed that she had revealed to Travis that I talked about him.

"Really?" he said with a question, looking back at me, and then over to Mary. I thought I detected a slight blush on his cheeks as well. "All good things I hope," he said with a laugh. He had crossed his arms over his chest now, I could see how muscular his forearms looked.

"Oh yes," Mary told him. "Definitely all good things."

"I would love to stay here and chat with you Sophie, but I'm tending bar tonight for my Mom, and it looks like they need me back there," Travis said to me, with disappointment on his face. I glanced over at the bar and saw two of the waitresses frantically waving to him. "Do you think... do you think you could come over to the bar to see me before you left?" he asked me.

My heart practically jumped out of my chest.

"Sure, I think I could do that," I said to him, trying to sound casual about it.

"That would be great," Travis said. I could feel him looking deeply into my eyes as I stared back at him. "I'll talk to you later then," he said to me. "It was nice to meet you, Mary," he said to Mary as he tapped his hand on the table.

"Great to meet you, Travis," Mary said, trying to contain herself.

I watched Travis walk away towards the bar. He met the two waitresses and took their orders right away, and I couldn't help but notice he was staring at me the whole time he was making the drinks they needed.

I looked over at Mary. Her mouth was hanging open a bit and then she broke out in a smile as I took a sip of my wine.

"Oh my God Sophie," she said to me in a hushed tone. " He is so hot! How did you walk away from that?"

I had to agree with Mary. Travis looked better than he ever had in the past. "Well, he was handsome back then, but now..." I heard my voice trailing off as I looked at him again. I could see him smile at me from behind the bar as he poured a beer for a patron. "Anyway, there were other circumstances involved back then. Things are different now."

"They sure are," Mary said as she turned and looked over at the bar. She turned back to face me. "He can't take his eyes off you, Sophie."

I don't think I had ever felt happier in my life. Mary and I kept staring at him until Patty came over and broke up the party with our food.

"Burger medium," she said, sliding the plate in front of Mary, "and a Cobb salad with house dressing," she said, placing the plate in front of me. Patty saw us staring at Travis behind the bar.

"Oh yeah, the bartender tonight," she said as she turned and stared as well. "That's Maggie's son Travis. He's pretty hot, and a real sweetheart too. All the girls have been swooning over him all night long. I hear he is single too," Patty said with more than a little interest. I could feel my jealousy rearing up again.

"Is that so?" Mary said to Patty as she picked at her fries.

"Yeah," Patty said as she squatted down next to the table to talk to us more privately. "his daughter is working with us tonight too. She's sweet. He's raised her all on his own. He'd be quite a catch." Patty sighed as she looked over at Travis.

"Patty," I interrupted her gaze, " can I get a glass of water please?" I said to her curtly.

"Sure Ms. Ingram, no problem," Patty said as she rose from her crouch and headed off to the kitchen.

"Looks like you have competition," Mary said sarcastically.

I slowly picked at my salad, finding it hard to concentrate on my meal at all. I kept glancing over at the bar to see what Travis was doing. Most of the time he was just chatting up the customers behind the bar, getting their drinks, keeping them happy. He would look over my way when he had a lull behind the bar, I would find myself quickly looking down at my food every time he did it.

"You're acting like you're one of the girls in our classes," Mary said to me as she finished polishing off her burger.

"I… I can't help it," I said to her, admitting how I was feeling. I couldn't get over the fact that he was here, he saw me, and he wanted to talk to me later. How was I going to manage to wait the whole time until there was a lull in the restaurant?

"I guess we'll be ordering dessert tonight," Mary said with a laugh.

"And coffee too," I told her. "Lots of coffee."

15

Travis

The night couldn't end fast enough for me. Every time I looked up from the bar, I could see Sophie sitting there, watching me, smiling at me. It made it difficult for me to concentrate on anything else, like making sure everyone got their drinks. It had been a long while since I was behind a bar outside of one of our firehouse parties, and the rust showed as people asked me for drinks that I used to know how to make without thinking about it. Thankfully, those moments were few and far between, and it was mostly a beer and wine crowd, so I was able to keep up pretty well.

My biggest worry now was what I was going to say to Sophie. I had asked her to stay so we could talk, and clearly, she and her friend Mary were just trying to string the evening along until I was free to meet with her, but I had no idea what I was going to say. I had appeared pretty confident when I went over to bring them their drinks, and I thought I held everything together pretty well. We both seemed to be in awe of each other, and I saw that at one point as she struggled for words as well. But now, when she would decide to come over, I needed to come up with something.

Sophie and Mary had been sitting there for hours now, having a slow dessert, coffee, more coffee, and then Mary started ordering drinks again. Even though the restaurant was thinning out, the bar still had few stools in use, so I was occupied. It was closing in on eleven, and I didn't know how much longer Sophie would be willing to wait. Mom usually closed up by midnight at the latest so it might not be too much longer.

A familiar face came in then and sat at the bar. It was Danny Seaver, a friend from high school who I hadn't seen in many years. He still looked the same as he did back when we were both on the wrestling team. Danny had been better than I was, stronger and faster, and won a couple of state titles along the way. He even got a scholarship to one of those big Midwest powerhouse wrestling schools, but he blew out his knee in one match in his junior year, and that was the end of him. Mom had told me a while back that he had a successful contracting business in town now and everyone local used his services.

"Travis?" Danny said to me as he sat at the bar and took off his ballcap. His brown hair was starting to thin a bit already even though he was my age. He stuck his hand out for me to shake it and I could feel he still had a very strong grip, and his calloused hands were a clear sign he worked hard each day.

"Hey Danny, it's great to see you," I said to him as I poured a beer and handed it off to the guy two seats away from him.

"What are you doing here?" he asked quizzically. "I haven't seen you in Canon for years."

"Yeah I was back in town to see my Mom and take care of a few things, and she needed some help at the bar tonight, so here I am."

Danny indicated he wanted a beer, so I poured him a lager into a pint glass and passed it over to him.

"How're things going?" he asked as he sipped his beer. "I heard you were a fireman over in Ridgefield."

"I was," I told him. "I got hurt on the job a few months back, and I had to retire." That was the first indication I had given to anyone that I was going to retire. It was odd to hear myself say it out loud, but I guess I had to get used to it.

"That sucks," Danny said. "Any ideas of what you are doing next?" He took another long sip of beer.

"Not really," I said, shaking my head. "I have my pension and disability, so we'll be okay. I have some time yet. Besides, I have to do some work on my Dad's house too."

"Oh that's right," Danny told me, looking serious. "I heard about your Dad; I'm sorry about that."

"Thanks, Danny." There was a bit of an awkward silence between us as he sipped his beer some more.

"What needs to be done at your Dad's?" he asked me. "I may be able to help you out."

"Mom had told me you were a contractor and doing really well," I said to him.

Danny smiled proudly back at me. "We're the best in town," he said as he handed me a pen imprinted with Seaver Contracting Services on it. 'So what does the house need?"

"Surprisingly not that much," I said to him. "it looks like it's mostly exterior stuff. The interior looks practically brand new."

"Wow, I'm surprised," Danny said, then felt a bit embarrassed about his comment about my Dad. "Nothing against your Dad, but he never seemed like the DIY guy to me or one that tended to house really well. I know that's an older house, so I'm surprised it looks so good. I'd be happy to take a look around the place for you if you want, see what it might need."

"That would be great, Danny, thanks." I was grateful for the help, particularly since I knew with my bum leg I might not be able to do much myself. "Should I call your office Monday?" I asked as I looked at the pen.

"Nah," he said to me. "I can meet you over there tomorrow morning if you want. It won't take long just to check things out. Consider it a favor for an old wrestling buddy," he told me with a smile.

We spent a few minutes talking about our lives in between me pouring drinks for the few patrons left. Danny was single, divorced a few years ago from a girl he had met in college and brought back to Canon with him. They had two kids that lived with her a couple of states over that he rarely saw. I told him about my exploits with Brenda and how I had Abby now, pointing her out to him proudly as she bussed tables. It was then he noticed me staring over at Sophie.

"Sophie Ingram, huh?" he said as he saw the look I gave her. "Didn't you two have a thing years ago?"

"Yes, we did," I mumbled, trying to focus on the conversation again. I leaned closer to Danny. "Say, Danny, do you know if she has been seeing anyone?"

"Sophie?" he said and laughed lightly. "I know plenty of guys who have knocked on that door, but she never answers. To be honest, it's surprising to see her out around town. She pretty much keeps to herself. Why? You thinking of trying to start up with her again?"

"I was thinking about it," I said to him confidently. I looked over at Sophie again and saw her smile again.

"Well, she seems interested in you," Danny said with a laugh.

Just then, Mom came over behind the bar.

"Last call folks," she said loudly, much to the disappointment of the few people left at the bar. Most of them headed out right away as Mom walked down to Danny and me.

"Hi, Danny," Mom said to him.

"Nice to see you, Maggie," Danny told her. "It's hard to believe you were able to drag him back to town," Danny said to her.

"It was easier to get him to do his homework when you two were younger," she told him with a smirk as she elbowed me.

I looked up from the bar and saw Sophie walking over towards us. I stood up straight as she came over and stood next to Danny and me.

"Travis," she said to me nicely. "I think I need to go. Mary's had a bit too much, and I'll have to drive her home in her car and then walk home from there. Is there any time for a quick chat?" she looked at me hopefully.

"I'm… I'm not sure if I have to clean up around the bar," I said as I tried to think fast to give myself to go over what I wanted to say to her.

"I can take care of the bar," Mom said to me as she smiled at me.

I was out of excuses. Danny then stepped up and interjected.

"I'd be happy to give Mary a ride home," he said to Sophie and me.

"Oh that's sweet of you Danny," Sophie said. "I don't want to trouble you."

"No trouble at all; I'm glad to do it. Mary lives over on Kelsey Place, right?" he asked as he got up from his stool.

"That's right," Sophie said to him. "How did you know?"

"Well, it's a long story," he said, looking down and feeling a bit embarrassed. "Let's just say we went out once or twice and leave it at that. I'll go corral Mary and get her home. You two have a nice talk. I'll see you tomorrow morning around nine, Travis?"

Danny broke me from my trance of staring at Sophie. "Yeah, nine is perfect. Thanks for your help, Danny." I said as I looked over at him.

"My pleasure," he said. "You two have a good night now."

We both watched as Danny went over to Mary and helped her out of her chair, putting one of his big arms around her small waist so he could guide her out the front door.

I looked around the restaurant and saw the place had cleared out. Some of the wait staff and bus staff were clearing the tables, including Abby.

"Well I guess I'm walking home from here," Sophie said to me with a light laugh.

I nervously placed a bar towel on the bar. Mom nudged my elbow and pointed at Sophie with her chin.

"I can walk you home," I said to Sophie.

"That… that would be nice," she told me as she pulled her purse over her shoulder.

"You two go on," Mom said to us from behind the bar. "I'll get Abby home with me when we are done here, Travis. Take your time."

"Thanks, Mom," I said as I walked from around the bar and stood next to Sophie.

"Shall we?" I pointed towards the door. As we were walking out together, I passed by Abby clearing a table and patted her on the head. She looked up at me and smiled.

"See you later Dad," she said to me, her voice sounding a little tired.

I held the front door open for Sophie to walk out ahead of me. Even though it was August, the air had gotten noticeably cooler than what it was this afternoon. The streets were very quiet, with all the local stores long closed and most people home and in bed hours ago. Sophie and I walked along in silence for a few steps.

"Your daughter seems very sweet," Sophie said to me, trying to start a conversation.

"Oh, you met Abby?" I asked her. She just nodded as we walked along. "Yes, she's a great kid. A little challenging at times lately, but overall she's great."

'Well, girls that age tend to be something of a challenge," Sophie replied. "Trust me, I see dozens of them a day. There are lots of highs and lows."

"Wonderful," I said to Sophie. She just laughed at me.

"It seems like you're doing a great job so far, you should be proud of yourself," she told me as we reached the corner of the street.

"Thanks,' I said to her humbly. It was just then I realized I had no idea where we were walking to.

"Where is your place?" I asked.

"Oh, I'm just over here on Hodges," she said to me. "I bought the old Gilbert place when Mr. Gilbert finally moved out."

"I remember Mr. Gilbert," I said to her fondly. "He owned the hardware store, right?"

"He did," Sophie said with a nod, looking down. "I figured if I was buying a house I was going to get it from someone I knew took good care of it before me so I wouldn't have to do much."

"You always were smart, Sophie," I said to her fondly as we walked. I kicked a loose stone on the sidewalk.

"Not always," she said quietly.

We made a left onto Collins Drive and started walking down towards the end of the street where Dad's, now my, house was. We stayed quiet for a bit until we got close to the house. Sophie looked up at the house and then over at me.

"So what's happening with your Dad's place?" she asked me as we got close to the fence around the front yard.

"Well, he left it to me," I told her casually. "I'm not really sure what to do with it just yet. Danny's going to come have a look at it tomorrow for me to see what it might need."

"It's yours huh?" Sophie seemed to brighten a bit as we walked further. "Does that mean that you'll be sticking around for a while?" There seemed to be a hint of hope in her voice.

"I don't know yet," I said to her as we crossed the street over to Hodges. "Maybe."

A few short steps later we were standing in front of her house.

"This is me," she said as she pointed to the front porch. "Thanks for walking me home Travis. It was wonderful to see you tonight." She turned as if she was going to walk away and up the porch.

It's now, or never, I said to myself.

"Sophie," I called to her. She turned around and came down the two steps she had climbed as I walked closer to her.

"Would you like to get together tomorrow night? You know, to catch up? I'd be happy to take you to dinner," I said to her.

"The only place worth eating dinner around here is either your Mom's place or the pizza place, and I've been to your Mom's two nights in a row. Besides, it gets awful noisy in there on Saturday nights."

I felt like she was rejecting me, and was disappointed in her answer.

"How about you come over here tomorrow night?" she said to me, looking up at me with a smile. "I can fix us some dinner, and we can talk some more."

"That sounds perfect," I said to her, feeling relieved.

"Okay," Sophie said, feeling perky again. "Let's say around six?"

"I'll be here," I said to her as she walked back up the porch.

"Good night Travis," I watched Sophie open the screen door and then her front door as she went inside. I stood outside her house for a minute, staring at it, feeling exhilarated. I saw Sophie peek out from behind the curtain in her living to look at me, and then she quickly drew the curtains closed again.

I turned and started walking back, realizing my car was back at the Homestead so I would need to go back and get it. The walk back to the restaurant seemed to take no time at all as my thoughts were occupied with how well things turned out today. Before I knew it, I was in the parking lot getting to my car as Mom and Abby were locking up the front door and coming out.

"Your back already?" Mom said to me, acting worried that I wasn't gone long enough.

"I just walked her home Mom," I said as I unlocked my car. I could see in Abby's face that she was tired from working hard.

"How did your night go, kiddo?" I said to Abby as I gave her hug.

"Great," she said to me through her yawn. "It was hard work, but I made fifty dollars in tips," she said to me, impressed by what she got.

"That reminds me," Mom said as she handed me an envelope. "Here's your share of the bar tips from today."

"You don't have to give me anything Mom," I said, trying to reject the envelope.

"Take it; you earned it," she replied, pushing the envelope back to me. "You did great work tonight," she said to me.

"If you don't want it, I'll take it," Abby said to me, looking up at me with sleepy eyes.

"Nevermind," I said to Abby, stuffing the envelope in my pocket.

"So how did it go with Sophie?" Mom asked as she leaned against the hood of my car.

"Fine," I said to her.

"Fine? That's it? That's all you have to say?"

I smiled at my mother wryly. "We're having dinner tomorrow night at her place."

Abby looked up at me, suddenly appearing awake. "You have a date?"

"Yeah, I guess I do," I said as I rubbed her head.

"Good job, Dad," Abby said as she hugged me again.

"Thanks, Abby." I hugged her back and shooed her to get into the car.

"What I am supposed to do for a bartender tomorrow?" Mom asked me.

"Are you serious?" I said to her, worried that she needed help tomorrow.

"I'm messing with you, Travis," she told me, pushing me to get into the car. "Boy, you need to work on your sense of humor before your date tomorrow. I can work the bar tomorrow, no problem."

I got into the front seat of the car and turned the engine on. "Do you want a ride back to the house?" I asked Mom.

"No, I always walk, you know that," she said with a smile. "I love to enjoy the peace of the town this time of night. Makes me realize why I love living here. I'll be home in a few minutes."

I pulled out of the parking lot and turned to head back towards Mom's house. Abby was already practically asleep by the time I made the turn. I passed Mom walking down the sidewalk, by the dry cleaner just down the street, and waved to her. She casually waved back as I drove on.

"Today was a good day," Abby mumbled to me as she turned towards me, eyes closed.

"Yes, it was," I answered her as I stroked her hair with my right hand.

16

Sophie

For the last few days, a good night of sleep seemed pretty elusive for me. At least last night I had a good reason to have trouble falling asleep. I was so excited by what had taken place between Travis and me that I couldn't think of anything else. The previous day had gone about as well as it could, right down to Travis walking me home. The only thing that would have made it better is if he had bent down to kiss me goodnight, but I guess that was too much to ask when we hadn't seen each other for fourteen years.

By seven AM I was wide awake and trying to plan out my day. I had just under eleven hours before he would be here again, and I wanted to make sure everything was perfect for our date. I checked around the house, cleaning up what little I had to put away. Since it was just me at home, there wasn't much of a mess at all to worry about. I threw some laundry on, put a few things away, and ran the vacuum over the floor just to make things a bit better.

As I stood looking around and admiring the clean house, I realized I didn't have anything to cook for dinner that night. Most nights I ate pretty lightly, and a quick look at my fridge let me know that unless Travis wanted yogurt and lemonade for dinner, I was going to need to go to the store.

I started to panic even more when I realized I had nothing nice to wear that night either. I had worn my best dress last night, and after rifling through my dresser drawers and closet, I fell back on the bed feeling panicked about what to wear. I needed to call in reinforcements for help.

I decided to send Mary a text message, a simple "I need your help!" to get her attention. I was going to call her, but I figured she probably was feeling a bit hungover from last night and maybe a ringing phone would not put her in the best of moods to start her day. I was more than surprised when she answered me right away, saying she would be here as fast as she could. Since it was only eight in the morning, she must have been feeling a lot better.

I was still wearing my pink t-shirt and pajama shorts about forty-five minutes later when I heard a car pulling up out in front of my house. I looked out the front window and saw a pickup truck there coming to a stop. I looked a little closer and could see the words "Seaver Contracting" on the side of the truck. Mary got out of the passenger side, wearing a blue t-shirt, denim shorts, and dark sunglasses, and closed the door to the truck. I saw Danny pull away as Mary made her way up the walk to my front door.

I opened the front door before she had a chance to knock and greeted her with a smile. She pulled open the screen door and brushed past me.

"Do you have coffee made?" she asked as she made her way into the kitchen.

"You know where the pot is," I told her as I followed her in and sat down at my kitchen table.

Mary poured herself a cup of coffee and slumped into the chair across from me, still wearing her sunglasses.

"How are you feeling?" I asked her, trying not to laugh.

"Oh, just peachy," she said to me snidely. "This is all your fault, you know." She took a big sip of coffee and placed the mug down on the table.

"How is this my fault?" I replied, wondering what I had done.

"If we didn't have to spend all night at the restaurant waiting on Mr. Wonderful, I wouldn't have drunk so much and..."

"And just what is it that you did, Mary?" I said, waiting smugly for a reply. "Or should I say who?"

Mary looked up at took her sunglasses off, revealing the dark circles under her eyes. I tried to stifle a laugh.

"If you had driven me home, Danny would never have been there," she said, trying to defend herself.

"I didn't make him stay with you; that was all on you," I retorted.

"It's fine," Mary answered, taking another sip of coffee. "After I threw up on him we had a great time."

Mary went on to explain to me that as he was helping her out of his truck last night, she threw up all over his jacket, shirt, and shoes. She apologized profusely to him, threw up again on the bushes in front of her house, and then he helped her inside. She offered to wash his clothes for him, he said no, and he helped her get upstairs. She woke up early in the morning and found him sleeping on the couch, and one thing led to another after that.

"Mary! You didn't!" I said, shocked that she would do that.

"Oh, stop Sophie," she said to me. "We had dated a few times awhile back and had fun, I just didn't want a serious boyfriend, so I stopped seeing him. He's very nice, has muscles in all the right places, and knows how to use them," she said with a grin.

"How did things go with you and Prince Charming?" she asked as she had more coffee.

I went into all the details of our walk home, and how I asked him over for dinner tonight.

"So all you did was walk home?" she said, astounded. "No deep talk, no kiss goodnight, no taking you on the kitchen table?"

I blushed at the thought. "No none of that. But Travis is coming over tonight, and I have nothing to make for dinner, and I have nothing to wear that looks nice. I really need your help, Mary, please."

Mary let out a deep sigh, took a sip of coffee, and then put her mug down.

"Fine," she said to me. "Go take a shower and get ready. By the time you are done, Simmons should be open. We'll see what we can find for you."

I went over to the other side of the table and hugged her and kissed her on top of the head. She placed her hand quickly on top of her head.

"Easy," she said to me, wincing a bit. "My hair hurts."

I laughed and raced upstairs to shower quickly. I went through my routine as fast as I could, put on my basics with a simple t-shirt and jean shorts, and came back downstairs without wasting time. Mary was on the couch, her left arm draped over her eyes, trying to protect them from the sunlight coming through the front window.

"You ready?" I said to her, having trouble standing in one place.

Mary peered over her arm and looked at me, and then slowly came to a sitting position. She slowly got to her feet.

"I guess so," she told me. "Let's go."

We walked out of the house, and both realized neither one of us had a car to drive. Mary's car was back at the Homestead and mine was still at the school. They were both about the same distance from my house, so we decided to walk over to the school and get my car since Mary didn't feel up to driving. She barely felt up to walking too and moved the entire way slowly to school. More than once I had to wait for her to catch up to me, and the school is only a few blocks away.

We finally got to the school and my car, the only one in the parking lot on a Saturday in the summer. I unlocked the doors with my remote and Mary climbed in the passenger side. I hopped in behind the wheel and slammed the door shut, causing Mary to flinch and give me a dirty look.

I drove over to Simmons Department Store, the only store of its kind in Canon and the one that pretty much everyone shopped at when they needed something that wasn't food. When we got there, it was a little after ten, and they were open for business. The parking lot, which was the largest in town, was already was about half full. There were lots of parents milling around, getting items for their kids at the back-to-school sales they were running.

Simmons was not only the only department store in town, but it was the tallest building outside of the town hall. It had three floors to comb through, making it the only place in town with an escalator. Mary and I walked in, and the bright lights of the store made her put her sunglasses back on right away. We walked over to the escalator to go up to the third floor where the women's department was.

A few other women were moving around the area where the dresses were, but other than that the area was pretty empty. Mary and I started looking through the racks of dresses to find something appropriate for the night. I was browsing through items, but I really had no idea what to look for or what would be best to get.

Mary held up a couple of dresses to me that seemed either obscenely short or too gaudy in style. She immediately rejected the few I offered up as being too conservative or prudish, even if I thought they looked pretty enough. We seemed to be at a stalemate when one of the salesgirls on the floor came over to us. She looked to be in her twenties, wearing a white blouse with maroon slacks, and a nametag that read "Penny." Penny was a tall brunette who seemed even taller with the heels she was wearing, making me feel a bit intimidated by her presence.

"Can I help you ladies with something?" she inquired, sounding professional and perhaps just a bit condescending. Mary took notice and stepped right up to her.

"Hi, Penny," Mary said, glancing over at her nametag and then looking up to her. "My friend Sophie here has a big date tonight and is looking for a dress. She needs something pretty, fun, and flirty, but not slutty. What have you got for her?"

I suddenly felt even smaller than before in front of Penny. I could feel her eyes looking me up and down as she walked a small circle around me.

"Size 6?" she said to me, sounding more like she was telling me than asking me.

"Yes," I replied shakily, feeling a bit violated that she could be so accurate just with a look.

"I think I have a few things that might be right for you," Penny said with a smile. "Why don't you head over to the dressing room and I'll bring you some things to try on?"

I just nodded blindly and grabbed Mary's hand and dragged her with me to the dressing rooms. There was a row of rooms, with no one in any of them, so Mary opened up the door to the first one. It was much larger than I had imagined it would be, with a pedestal in the center of the room surrounded by three mirrors.

"Up on the pedestal, Princess," Mary said to me with a grin.

"Very funny," I said to her. I paced around the room a bit, trying to get over my anxiety when Penny walked in holding three dresses.

"Let's start with these," she said, hanging them on a rolling rack just inside the door to the room. I could see that one was white, one was red, and one was purple, but beyond that, I couldn't make out the details. Mary walked over to the dresses and looked at them. She held the purple one up, and I immediately shook my head no. She placed it back on the rack, leaving the red and the white. The red looked cute, a skater dress that was sleeveless with a high neckline and a small cutout on the back near the waistline. The skirt part of the dress had a cute flare to it. I decided I would give that one a try.

Mary then held up the white dress. The white dress was also a skater style knit dress with a flared skirt, but this one had princess seams. The neckline was a small V to show some cleavage, and I wasn't sure how I felt about that one. I liked the white, but I didn't want to seem too forward since it was our first date in fourteen years. Mary was nodding insistently, so I knew I had to try it on.

Mary brought the white one over to me and handed it to me. I kicked my sneakers off and then took a look at Penny. She was standing just inside the dressing room door looking at us. I think she got the hint from our stares that I would be comfortable undressing if she left.

"I'll be right outside if you need help," she said to as she turned and walked out, shutting the door behind her.

"She's charming," Mary said to me with a sneer.

"She's just doing her job," I said to her as I unzipped my shorts and stepped out of them. I then took off my t-shirt and held my hand out for Mary to hand me the dress. She just stared at me standing there.

"What?" I said to her, holding my hand out for the dress.

"Sophie, please, I am begging you, don't wear those tonight."

"Wear what?"

"That bra and those panties look like something my mother wore ten years ago," she said with disdain.

I looked at myself in the mirror and didn't see anything wrong.

"They're comfortable," I said in my defense.

"Of course they're comfortable," Mary said. "you've been wearing them for so long they would have to be at this point. You want something pretty tonight. Something that will make you feel confident, feminine and girly. Something you wouldn't be embarrassed about Travis seeing."

I blushed lightly. "I don't know that anyone is seeing my underwear tonight," I said defensively.

"Soph, you love this guy, you've waited fourteen years for him to come back, and to put it bluntly, you're a virgin that hasn't had a date in a long time. Your body is crying out to be seen by someone besides you." Mary stood there holding the white dress, waiting for me to say okay.

"Fine," I gave in. "I could use a new bra I guess."

"Great," she said to me. "Oh, Penny," Mary shouted. Penny came in before I could even cover up.

"Yes?" Penny asked.

Mary walked over to Penny and put her arm around her.

"Penny, my friend here needs a new bra and panty set. Something pretty, functional and just a hint of sexy."

Penny walked over to me again and was staring at my chest. I was growing uncomfortable again when she said, "34B. I'll get you some choices to go with the white and the red."

I watched Penny walk out of the dressing room.

"That's amazing," I said to Mary as I stood there.

"The girl has some talent, I must admit," Mary said with a laugh.

Moments later, Penny knocked on the dressing room door and came in with some bra choices with matching panties. I looked at a few of the bras, and none of them seemed right to me until I hit upon the white demi bra with some lace on the edge of the cups. It looked pretty and looked like it might give me the bit of "boost" I wanted without being too revealing. I decided to try that one on and turned away from Mary and Penny as I took my bra off and put this one on. Once I got the straps in place, I turned to Mary and Penny. Penny came right up to me and made some adjustments on the straps and the cups, taking my breasts in her hands to adjust things properly. I was stunned, but when she was done, I had to admit the bra looked better.

"Yes!" Mary shouted. "Nicely done, Penny. That's the bra you need, Sophie."

I felt prettier and sexier than I had in a long time and pulled the white dress on over my head. I did up the zipper on the back and turned around, giving the ladies a look. They both smiled at what they saw, and then Mary gave Penny a high-five. I looked in the mirror and fell in love with what I saw.

"This is the one," I said lightly as I turned, watching the skirt flounce lightly.

I decided to take the dress, the bra, and the matching panties, and Mary and Penny talked me into getting the red dress too, so I had more than one to wear for now. I ended up getting matching undergarments for that as well, along with a pair of red heels to match the red dress and some white flats for the white dress. My credit card wasn't going to know what hit it, but since I never splurged on myself for anything, this felt right.

Penny rang everything up and had loosened up a bit by the time we were leaving, asking me to come back and let her know how everything had worked out on the date. Mary and I left with my purchases in tow, and I had a smile on my face, feeling a bit better since I knew I had something nice to wear.

We were then off to Gallagher's Market two blocks over to figure out what to get for dinner. I was confident in my cooking, but I also wanted to make sure everything went well, and Travis enjoyed the meal. I knew years ago he was a steak guy, so I figured that was the safest bet and went over to the meat counter. Jim Gallagher, one of the four sons of Colin Gallagher, the owner, was behind the meat counter when we arrived.

"Hello, Sophie… Mary," he said to us, those his eyes brightened a bit more when he saw Mary.

Mary smiled back at him as I glanced over at her.

"Jimmy," I said to him. " I need two ribeye steaks, please."

"Ribeyes?" Jim sounded surprised. "What's the occasion, Sophie? Usually, it's just chicken for you."

"Hot date tonight," Mary said to him, as she leaned forward on the counter to get closer to Jim.

"Really? With who?" Jimmy said to her, speaking to her instead of me.

"Travis Stone, Maggie's son," Mary said, running her index finger on Jim's left arm. Jim looked like he was in a trance.

"I don't think I know him," Jim said, staring into Mary's eyes.

"Well he's been out of town for a long time, but he and Sophie used to have a thing," she whispered to him. "Do you think you could set her up with something really good Jim, for me?" Mary was batting her eyelashes at him as she talked to him.

"Sure thing," he said as he stepped back. "I'll cut you two good ones, Sophie. I'll be back in a minute." Jim stepped into the back room to get my steaks while Mary looked over at me.

"You're shameless," I said to her.

"Oh come on, Sophie," Mary chided. "A little flirting is fun. Try it with Travis tonight, you'll see. He'll love it."

Jim came back out and handed me two steaks, nicely wrapped in brown butcher's paper.

"Anything else ladies," Jim said proudly, staring at Mary.

"I think that's it Jimmy, thank you," I said to him as I started to walk away.

"Thanks, Jimmy," Mary said as she blew him a kiss and moved with me. As we walked, Mary whispered to me, "Is he staring at me?" I took a quick glance back and saw Jimmy's eyes following her down the aisle.

"You bet he is," I answered.

"Good," Mary said with a wicked grin, wiggling her hips a bit more as we walked.

We picked up some potatoes and spinach, and I got the makings of a salad as well. I didn't think I would have time to make anything for dessert, but they had some great-looking pies at the bakery counter, so I picked up a blueberry pie for dessert. Mary had wandered over and chosen a six-pack of beer for me to have on hand in case Travis wanted something.

I paid for my purchases, and we hauled the bags out to the car. All in all, it was an expensive day so far, and we had spent several hours doing the shopping. The day that started at nine had already run to one in the afternoon. I only had five hours before the date.

I drove over to the Homestead parking lot so Mary could pick up her car. We pulled in next to where her car was parked.

"Thanks for your help today Mary," I said to her. "I really needed it."

"No problem Sophie," she said, sounding sincere. She then turned to face me and gave me a big sister-type look.

"Now what?" I said to her, trying to figure out what I may have forgotten.

"Sophie," she said in a serious tone, "I'm not saying anything is going to happen or should happen tonight, but if it does... do you know what to, you know, do?"

"Mary, I do not want to have this conversation," I said to her, turning my head forward. "My mother gave me "the talk" when I was thirteen. I think I remember it."

"Well your mother may have told you the basics about how babies are made, but there's more to it than one thing goes in the other," she said bluntly.

"Mary, I'm 32. I've read lots of books, seen movies and, believe it or not, have done some things myself. Just because I'm a virgin doesn't mean I don't know anything." I was feeling a little put out.

"I'm sorry Sophie," she said sincerely. "I didn't mean to offend you. I just want your first time… if it is your first time… to be a good experience. For a lot of people, it isn't, and you're a good person. You deserve it to be."

"Awww, thanks, Mary," I said as we hugged. "I appreciate the thought, but I'm not counting on anything like that happening tonight. It's the first time we're together in a long time. We have a lot to talk about I think before anything like that might happen."

"Fair enough," she said to me as she got out of the car and closed the door. Mary leaned her head in the open window. "Have a good time tonight. I want all the details tomorrow," she said pointing a finger at me.

"Okay," I said with a smile.

Mary got in her car as I backed out of the parking spot and began the short ride home to my house. I had a lot of preparing to do before Travis showed up.

17

Travis

I got to my dad's… my house by about 8:30 so I would have some time to look around before Danny arrived. I walked around the outside, surveying the house a little closer than I had the first time I was here with Abby. The outside definitely needed some work. The gutters needed to be replaced, the porch needed some boards replaced and a new paint job, and the outside of the house looked like it could use some fresh paint as well. The yard was a decent size since it was a corner lot, and there was plenty of mowing that needed to be done, something I didn't know how I would feel up to with my leg.

It's funny how things could change in life so quickly. Before that last fire call, everything was going smoothly, I was in perfect health, and might have even thought of myself as a pretty rough and tumble guy. I wasn't scared of anything, never hesitated to make a move, and made decisions easily. Ever since that fire, the events and the injury, I didn't feel the same. I second-guessed myself with nearly everything, from what groceries to buy to how to deal with Abby to even figuring out if I should back here to Canon for all this. Even when I first got back to town, I didn't know what direction anything was taking, but somehow, after seeing Sophie last night, it feels like things are starting to fall back into place.

I sat down on the front steps as I waited for Danny to arrive. The steps creaked underneath me as I sat and I took a look around the area. It was peaceful, and the few people that were walking the sidewalk all said hello, waved or nodded, even if they didn't know who I was. Maybe this was the kind of life I was ready for, and the kind of life Abby needed now.

I looked up, staring out into the street, and saw Danny's truck go flying by the house in the direction towards Sophie's place just down the street. I wondered if maybe he forgot where the house was, but just a minute later, here he was, coming back from the other direction, and he pulled into the driveway right behind my car.

Danny hopped out of the car and stretched as he slowly walked over to me. I couldn't help but notice that it looked like he was wearing the same outfit he wore last night.

"Morning, Travis," he said to me as he came up to me sitting on the steps.

"Hey Danny," I said to him, covering up my eyes a bit as I squinted at him as he stood in the sunlight. " I thought maybe you forgot where the house was. I saw you go by here and then come back around."

"Oh, that," he said, grinning at me. "No, I remember where the house was. I just had to drop Mary off at Sophie's." Danny reached up and tugged at his cap a bit.

"Really," I said trying not to sound as surprised as I was.

"Don't get the wrong idea, Travis," he said to me defensively. "I would never take advantage of a situation like that. I drove her home, and helped her into the house and was getting ready to go when she looked like she needed someone watching her. I helped her upstairs and made myself comfortable on the couch downstairs, like a gentleman. When I woke up in the morning, she was there standing next to the couch, barely dressed and smiling at me, saying she wanted to thank her hero for getting her home." Danny smiled a shy smile. " She's a heck of a woman," he said. "Anyway, how'd things go with you and Sophie?" he asked me.

"Oh, I just walked her home. We talked a little bit, but not much. I'm going to her place for dinner tonight though," I said proudly.

"Wow, good for you Travis." Danny sounded genuinely surprised. "I'm sorry if that sounded wrong," he said apologetically. "Sophie just doesn't have the reputation of dating much around here, so she must really want to see you if she's going out with you, nevermind inviting you over for dinner."

"I guess so," I said to him not knowing what else to say.

"So, let's take a look at the house," Danny said, slapping his hands together.

We walked around the exterior of the house for a bit, and Danny took a close look at everything; from the siding to the window frames and more. He even crawled under the porch in the front and the back to check the foundation.

"Well, it needs some help outside," he said to me as he wiped the dust off himself after getting out from under the front porch. "The foundation is sound, so that's good. You'll have to replace the gutters for sure, and I can't tell you about the roof until I get up there to look at it. That one window on the far side looks like it should be replaced so you may want to do them all at once to save yourself a headache. It definitely needs some new paint too, and you probably want to replace the front porch."

"Anything else?," I asked. It sounded like a lot of work to me.

"We still need to looking inside," Danny told me as he walked up to the front door. I walked over and unlocked the door, and we stepped inside. It was still hard to believe just how immaculate the place looked inside. Danny checked the wood floors as he made his way across the living room towards the kitchen. He checked the walls, the appliances, and the cabinets, and was impressed by what he found.

"So far everything looks pretty good," he said to me. "Some of this stuff is practically new, maybe less than a year old, so you're in good shape there."

I was relieved to hear that much as Danny made his way around the kitchen and through the doorway back into the hall. He went up the stairs to check the bedrooms up there, and I followed close behind him. He looked at both bedrooms and the bathroom upstairs, paying special attention to the smaller bedroom.

"This is all new in here Travis," He said to me.

"You mean the paint?" I asked him.

"Not just the paint, but the walls are new too. Someone put up all new sheetrock, probably new wiring too. And the flooring in here is new, too. They did nice work," Danny noted.

"I wonder who did it," I commented as we walked back down towards the stairs.

"I wish I knew,' Danny told me. "They're either good competition or someone I should hire," he said as we went down the stairs. He checked the bathroom in the hallway, and then came out.

"I have to tell you, Travis, the inside of this house is fantastic. I didn't see one thing I would change," he told me. "That will save you a bundle on the work to do. You thinking of fixing the place up and selling, or are you going to live here?"

I paused when he asked me that question.

"I haven't decided yet," I answered honestly.

"Well, I know houses don't sell for the high prices here like they do in other areas, but if we fix up the outside of this place, you could get good money if you wanted to sell. I don't think it would take long either," Danny said as he took his cap off and scratched his head.

"Of course," he then added, "it's the perfect place for just two people to live, or maybe three," he said as he grinned at me.

"Let's not get too far ahead of things Danny," I told him. "Sophie and I haven't seen each other in a long time, and… well, there's a lot of history to get passed still."

"I get it," Danny said to me. " Just seems like maybe it's fate to me. You come all this way, maybe looking for a new place to start, here's this house just waiting for you, and the girl you want in your life is here after all these years, lives down the street, and wants to see you? It doesn't get more perfect than that if you ask me."

"I guess we'll see how it goes," I said as I slapped him on the back and started walking towards the door. Danny followed me out onto the front porch as I turned and locked the door.

"No one locks doors in Canon, Travis," Danny said with a smile.

"Force of habit," I said to him as I turned the lock. "So can you get me an estimate for the work?" I asked him as we went down the creaky porch steps.

"Sure, I'll work something up for you. I can drop it off at your Mom's later today or tomorrow, and then if it works for you, maybe we can pick a day next week to start working. You should call Carl Peterson if you want someone to clean up this lawn for you. He can get his crew over here and make it all look nice," Danny said to me. We had reached his truck, and he opened the door and reached in and grabbed his leather case. He pulled out a card and handed it to me with Carl Peterson's number on it.

"Thanks, Danny," I said to him. "Thanks for everything."

"Glad I could help," he said as he got in his truck and started it up. "I'll get you that estimate. Enjoy your date tonight," Danny winked at me as he backed out of the driveway.

I took a quick look down at my watch and saw that it was only 10:30. I still had plenty of time before the date and figured I could get over to Mom's house and maybe catch a nap before I started getting ready.

I was back at Mom's house in no time at all and walked in. I called out to Mom and Abby, but they must have already left to go to the restaurant for the day.

I'm surprised Mom could get Abby out of bed, I thought to myself.

I slowly made my way up the stairs, feeling a twinge in my leg as I got to the top of the stairs. I had done more walking in the last two days than I had done since they had me doing physical therapy, and I was feeling it. I kicked my boots off and laid back on the bed, letting out a deep sigh. I closed my eyes, feeling the faint breeze in the room coming from the window. It was still a little early before it would get too hot outside, and the breeze felt good.

I tried to put all the thoughts out of my head so I could get some rest, but it seemed like every time I started to drift off, something would pop back in to catch my attention. Whether it was worrying about Abby, Mom, my job, our future, the house, Dad's secret life, or Sophie, there was always something there.

Eventually, my exhaustion got the better of me. I was dreaming, a good dream for a change. Sophie and I were together in Dad's, now my, house, sitting on the couch together, while Abby was on the floor with her headphones on, her head in a book. The three of us were there, happy... more so than I had been in a very long time. I slid my arm around Sophie and pulled her close to me, kissing her deeply, feeling her lips pressing softly against mine. We slowly broke the kiss, and I could see her smiling at me, telling me she loved me.

The dream seemed to just go on casually, with not much happening, as we moved through the house, having dinner, getting Abby off to bed, and then finally going to bed ourselves. I could see myself taking hold of her and making love to her like I had always wanted to but never got the chance to. She was so responsive and reciprocal with her moves and motions, and the whole experience was amazing. The passion was there, it was intense, and it felt so real that when I was jolted awake by the sound of a text message coming to my cell phone that I couldn't believe my bad luck for not getting to see it all through.

I glanced over at my phone and saw it was 4:30. The text message was from Abby:

"Have a good time on your date while I slave away working, LOL. Love you."

Even though we had been here for just a short time, Abby seemed much more relaxed and happier, and she was even talking to me more than she had in weeks.

Maybe this is the place for her, I thought.

I sat up in bed, feeling sweat on my body as the day had gotten warmer while I slept. I walked down to the bathroom to take a shower to start getting myself ready. I cleaned myself up quickly in the shower and glanced at myself in the mirror. I had a little more stubble today, but I liked the idea of not having to shave every day like I did when I was in the department. It made me feel a little more badass than I had been lately, so I decided to leave it. I splashed on a little cologne for good measure and walked back down the hall to get dressed.

I hadn't brought any fancy clothes with me for this trip, and it's not like I had that much you would consider fancy outside of the one suit I owned. Anyway, I didn't think I had any need for anything fancy, let alone that I would be going out on a date, so it was going to be jeans, a white button-down shirt, and my boots, and that was going to have to do.

It was about 5:15 and I was ready to go. I decided maybe it would be a good idea to pick up a bottle of wine, so I headed over to the one liquor store in town and picked up a bottle of pinot noir to bring along. I didn't know much about wine, but the lady in the liquor store seemed to think this was a good choice, so I went with it. As I walked out of the liquor store and was walking back towards my car, I passed Rainbow Bouquet, the local flower shop. I decided to head in and see if I could get some flowers for Sophie.

I walked into the small shop, the bells on the door jingling as I entered. I was hit with the sweet mix of floral smells as I made my way up towards the counter, where the woman behind the counter was putting together a bouquet for an older gentleman. The older man turned to look at me as I came up behind them, and he did a double take.

"Travis?" he asked, like he was greeting an old friend.

I had a little trouble placing who he was as he faced me.

"Yes?" I replied.
"I'm Fred Perkins, I own the dry cleaners down the street from your Mom's place," he said to me as he held out his hand for me to shake.

I took his hand and shook it, vaguely remembering the place since it was where my Mom always brought the uniforms for the restaurant.

"How are you Mr. Perkins," I said politely. " I apologize, I didn't recognize you. I haven't... I haven't been around much lately."

"Oh don't worry about it Travis," he said to me as I released his hand. " And call me Fred; you're a grown man now. It's nice to see you back in town. I'm sure it makes your mother very happy."

"Yes, I think it does," I replied as the woman coughed politely to get Mr. Perkins attention. She handed him the nicely wrapped bouquet of a mix of red roses and lilies.

"Nice arrangement," I said to him, pointing at the flowers.

A blush came across his cheeks. "Oh, these. Yes, well, hopefully, it will make her happy. You have a nice night, Travis." He said as he smiled and started to walk away.

"You too, Fred," I smiled and turned to the woman at the corner.

"He comes in every week and gets the same arrangement every Saturday," she said as she watched him walk out the door. "It's very sweet."

"Yes, it is," I said, thinking that it is nice that he does that.

"What can I help you with these evening?" she asked me as she cleared the counter off.

"Well... I have a date tonight, with someone special, and I wanted to get her some nice flowers," I said feeling a little embarrassed.

"It's nice to see some young men still think it's important to make a lady feel special," she said with a big smile. "Did you have anything in mind?"

"I know she likes daisies," I said to her.

At least she used to like daisies, I thought, hoping she still did.

"Okay," the woman said to me. I have some nice white daisies. How about if I mix in some pink roses and make a bouquet for you?"

"That sounds perfect, please," I responded.

She went over to her refrigerated case and got the daisies and pink roses out.

"Are six roses okay?" she asked me.

"I guess that's fine," I told her, not knowing what seemed right or not. I watched as she expertly arranged and cut the flowers, so they created a beautiful bouquet. She then wrapped the flowers in white floral paper and handed them to me.

"They look fantastic," I complimented her. I paid for the flowers and wished her good evening.

"Enjoy your date," she commented as I walked out.

It seems like everyone is wishing me a good date tonight.

I made my way to my car, placed the bottle of wine and the flowers on the front seat next to me, and looked down at my watch. It was 5:45, so I guessed it was time to head over to Sophie's.

Better get going now, so I don't get stuck in traffic," I said to myself with a laugh. I could already see some of the shops closing up for the night, and there were hardly any people on the streets, even though the sun was still shining brightly on the late August day.

I slowly drove over towards Sophie's place, passing my house on Collins as I went. I pulled up in front of her house and turned my car off. I got out and walked around to the passenger's side and opened the car door to take out the bottle of wine and the flowers. I closed the car door and looked up at Sophie's house. I could see the front door was open and could faintly hear some music playing, coming through the screen door and down the walkway.

I made my way up the walkway, and the front porch steps, hearing my boots scuffle on the boards beneath my feet. I knocked lightly on the screen door and waited for Sophie to reply.

Here we go.

18

Sophie

I had spent the rest of the afternoon getting the house ready, doing prep work for dinner and setting the table, then getting myself ready for the date. I went up and took another shower, even though I had taken one before Mary and I left to go shopping. I think it was more out of nerves than anything else. I made sure to dry myself off well and wrapped the towel around myself as I left the bathroom, just as always do. I was standing before the mirror at my vanity, looking at my reflection, when I smiled and impulsively tossed the towel to the side. I looked at my naked reflection in the mirror, something I rarely did and looked at my body. I felt good about how I looked, happy with my body and that I had kept myself in good shape.

My body looks pretty good, I thought to myself as I put my hands up into my hair, shaking it around a bit. I let my hands travel down my body, watching myself in the mirror the whole time, touching myself lightly. I closed my eyes and imagined Travis was standing there with me, standing behind me, and it was his hands gliding over my body. I could feel his strong hands starting at my shoulders and working their way down my arms, making the hair on my arms stand up and send shivers throughout my body. His hands would come to rest on my waist as he lightly rubbed his fingertips on my waist and hips. He would then wrap his arms around me as his hands came back up my body, cupping my breasts in each hand, squeezing them gently.

I could feel his hands slowly working their way back down me again, retracing their steps down my breasts to my waist, but this time they kept going lower. His fingertips grazed just inside my thighs, and I could feel myself shiver again from his touch. He touched me lightly, again and again on my thighs. I could feel his warm breath on my neck as he began to kiss me. His fingers moved slowly from the outer parts of my thighs in, getting closer and closer until I could feel them around me, before one finger, and then two, gently and easily slipped inside me and I gasped in delight. His left hand's fingers moving in me, the kisses on my neck, and then his right hand, oh his right hand, caressing my right breast. Everything was moving in such good rhythm, and my body was responding perfectly to each touch. Before I knew it, I could feel my body tensing on his fingers, and I felt a huge release inside me as he turned me around and kissed me on the lips, holding me tightly against his body.

I opened my eyes as my knees felt weak. I looked at my reflection and could see I was flush, nipples erect and my right hand lightly petting myself now after a tremendous orgasm. At first, I felt a little embarrassed having done that since I almost never touch myself like that, but it had been so long, and it felt so good, that I smiled back at my reflection and relished the way my body felt.

I sat down at the vanity, my legs still feeling wobbly, and I picked up some lipstick and applied just a light coat of red to my lips. I didn't put any other makeup on, though I grabbed my favorite perfume and gave myself a light spray of the lilac-scented liquid, so there was just a trace on my body.

When I felt like I had finally composed myself, I stood up and went over to the bags of clothing I had bought earlier today. I took out the white bra and panty and laid them on the bed, and then put the white dress next to it. I stepped into the panties and pulled them up my legs, feeling the cool satin against my body. I was used to just wearing cotton all the time and enjoyed the soft feeling against my body. The bra was next, and I put it on and made adjustments just like Penny did in the dressing room earlier at Simmons so that the bra fit perfectly and gave me just enough boost so that it would look good in my dress. I was already feeling more girly than I had felt in a long time.

I picked up the dress and lifted it over my head, letting it fall onto my body before zipping it up in the back. I turned to look in the mirror and could not believe what I saw. I loved the way the dress held my body, and just the hint of cleavage showing through maybe me feel just a tad naughtier than I had ever felt, particularly after what I had just done. I gave myself a small twirl in the dress, feeling the skirt spin beneath me. I slipped into the white flats I had purchased and knew the outfit was perfect.

I took a quick look over at my alarm clock and saw it was 5:30. Travis would be here soon, so I rushed downstairs to make sure everything looked just right.

I walked through the living room and flipped some music from my iPod on, trying to find something quiet, soothing and maybe just a tad romantic. The classical music would do for now, and I could always change it if Travis wanted to hear something else.

I got the potatoes ready to put in the oven, figuring on a simple baked potato to go with the steaks, and let the steaks rest on the counter so they could come to room temperature. The spinach would take just a few minutes to heat up, and before I chopped it a bit, I made sure to put my apron on so I wouldn't get anything on my dress. I quickly chopped up some shallot and parsley as well so I could put them in the pan after the steaks to make a quick butter sauce when they were done. I checked the table and saw it was set nicely. I thought about candles but quickly put them away, thinking that it was too formal. I wanted Travis to feel comfortable, without any pressure.

I heard a knock on the screen door and practically jumped in the air. I took a deep breath and walked towards the door and saw Travis standing there, smiling.

I opened the door, and Travis walked past me, still smiling. I got a quick whiff of the manly cologne he was wearing and felt my knees get weak again. I had forgotten how much I missed the smell of a man's cologne near me, and it had been a long time since I had experienced it.

I turned to look at Travis, standing in the living room in his long-sleeve shirt and jeans, the stubble on his face, and those amazing emerald eyes looking back at me.

"Right on time," I said to him as my mind was suddenly blank of what to say.

"I got these for you," Travis said to me, as he handed me the flowers, a beautiful mix of pink roses and white daisies.

"Oh, daisies. They're my favorite," I cooed as I inhaled the sweet aroma of the flowers. "You remembered," I said fondly.

"Yes," he said to me softly. "I remember at school I always used to steal them from the quad and bring them to your dorm room," he said with a laugh. "The groundskeeper used to chase me every time he saw me."

I laughed and went into the kitchen to put the flowers in a vase. I felt Travis' eyes follow me as I walked past him. I got the vase off the windowsill, put some water in it, and placed the flowers inside. I carried the vase back out to the living room and placed them on the small coffee table I had in front of the couch.

"Your house looks nice," Travis commented as he looked around.

"Thanks," I told him. "It's small, just two bedrooms, but it's perfect for me. Just the right space, a nice front porch, a small yard... that's all I really need."

We stood together in the living room, neither of us saying anything for a moment, just stewing in awkward silence.

"I can start dinner now if you want," I said to Travis, "or we could sit and relax for a little bit if you'd like."

"Let's sit for a bit," Travis answered as he sat down on the couch. I untied the apron in the back and pulled it over my head, leaving me in my white dress.

"Wow," Travis said as he stared at me. "You look... you look amazing."

I felt proud of myself as I blushed a bit and watched Travis' eyes travel over me in the dress.

"Why thank you," I said as I sat in the lounge chair just to the right of the couch, folding the skirt under me as I sat.

Travis sat back on the couch and winced a little as he crossed his right leg over his left.

"Are you okay?" I asked him, concerned.

"Oh, it's just my leg," he said to me. "I was injured during a fire a couple of months ago. I fell through a weak porch, and it tore up my leg pretty good. I was stuck in there, and they had to pull me out."

I gave Travis a look of concern. "That sounds terrifying," I said to him.

"It was scary," he told me, looking like he meant it. "It was a bad fire. We lost one of the guys in my company, and the woman who lived in the house with a little girl."

"Oh, Travis, that's terrible," I replied. "I'm so sorry. Was the little girl okay?"

He shifted on the couch, seeming uncomfortable with answering. "She was fine. I was able to get her out before anything happened."

"Then you're a hero," I said with a smile.

"Hardly," he told me, recoiling at the thought. "I was just doing my job. If I did it well, I would have saved two more lives."

I felt bad for him. "Sometimes... sometimes we can't save everyone, Travis, no matter how much we want to," I told him, reaching over and putting my left hand on his right knee.

Travis looked over at me and nodded. I slowly pulled my hand back and sat back, trying to think of something else to say. We had a lot of topics I wanted to cover, to help clear the air, but I didn't know where I should begin.

"Tell me a little about your daughter," I asked him nervously. I knew this was likely going to open things up, but we had to start somewhere.

"She's smart as a whip and twice as sassy," Travis said with a laugh. "in that respect, she is a lot like her mother was."

"Maggie said you raised Abby on your own," I mentioned. I could feel myself gripping parts of my skirt in my fingers, feeling nervous from all the questions.

" I did… I mean I have," Travis said as he sat forward a little bit. "Are you sure you want to hear about this Sophie?"

"I do," I said honestly. " I want to know what life has been like for you."

"Okay," Travis said as he sighed. "I met Brenda a few months after I started training to become a fireman. She was a waitress at the diner a bunch of us hung out in. She was young like me, barely nineteen. Brenda Flannery was her name. She was a pure Irish girl, through and through – the red hair, green eyes, freckles and the Irish brogue to boot. She had moved from Dublin when she was sixteen. One night we were there late and hung out at the diner all night long talking. One thing led to another, and we ended up back at her place, and, well…"

I looked down a little bit as he looked at me with his pause.

"A few weeks later she told me she was pregnant. For a while, she was fine with it. We moved in together, took Lamaze classes, set up space for the baby in our apartment, the whole works. I had just joined the department when Abby was born. I thought Brenda was happy with everything. She was home with the baby while I was working at the department nearby in Ridgefield, but it became apparent that she wasn't happy with how things were going. She would get frustrated with Abby and the crying, and the feedings and didn't really know what to do. Neither of us did really. We were just figuring it out as went along. One night when Abby was crying a lot, Brenda called me at the firehouse and told me I needed to come home, that she didn't know what to do."

Travis stood up from the couch and started pacing around.

"I got Abby to sleep when I got home, but Brenda was still hysterical. She said how she wasn't ready for this, she wasn't cut out for having a family. I tried to calm her down, and I thought it had worked. I went down to the coffee shop in the morning to get us some breakfast. I wasn't gone more than fifteen minutes. When I got back, our neighbor next door was sitting at our kitchen table holding Abby. She said Brenda said she needed to go and asked if she would watch her until I got back. I checked the bedroom, and she had taken most of her clothes and a few things, and all the cash we kept in the lockbox in the closet was gone. I asked some guys on the police force to try to track her down, but no one could ever find her. My guess is she went back to Ireland. She just decided she didn't want to be tied down anymore."

"Oh my God," I said. "That's terrible."

"I thought it was too at first," Travis said as he looked at me. "I didn't know how I was going to make it work. A single dad, a fireman, trying to raise a little girl. It wasn't easy, but I had good people around me at the firehouse, and they all worked with me those first few years to help out – giving me better hours, wives and girlfriends rotating to watch Abby, all kinds of stuff – and as time went on I think I became a pretty good father. Then she had to go and hit puberty, and all hell broke loose."

I laughed out loud at this. "You have probably heard this a million times Travis, but the teenage years don't get any better I'm afraid."

"So I have been told," Travis told me. He sat back down on the couch again and looked at me. "So tell me something about you," he asked. "What have you been up to all these years?"

"Wow," I said to him, shaking my head. "Nothing nearly as dramatic as you. After," I paused, trying to feel for my words, "After I went back to school, I finished up my teaching degree. I had every intention of going somewhere else to teach, somewhere away from here. I came home the summer after my graduation, and my mother was all proud I had my diploma. She asked me what was next and I told her what I wanted, and she wasn't thrilled about it. She thought I should come back here, give back to my community and stay with her. I didn't know what to do. I felt guilty about leaving her all by herself. The middle school here was looking for a new eighth-grade teacher, so I applied, and I got the job. You know, a hometown girl and all. Mom was happy, and the job was good. Six months later she tells me she was selling the house to move in with her sister down in Naples. I was stunned. Here I was, having changed my life for her, and now she was leaving. So she left about six months later and here I was teaching. I rented an apartment for a while until I saved up some money to buy a place, and here I am."

"Do you regret staying?" Travis asked me.

I thought about the question for a minute. "I think I did, at first. I know I looked at taking jobs at other places, bigger places. But then I saw how much I was bringing to the students here, and to the community here. I realized I was a big help to families here, just like I had wanted, except it was a small town, and I was happy with it. So I decided to stay, and I'm glad I did."

We sat quietly again for another minute before I broke the silence.

"Should I start dinner?" I asked Travis, as I stood up.

"Actually, I would rather keep talking if that's okay with you," he said to me. "But I could use something to drink."

"Oh, I'm sorry Travis; where are my manners?" I walked towards the kitchen. "What would you like? I've got lemonade, iced tea, and some beer for you if you want one."

"Beer would be great, thanks," he shouted back to me.

I opened a bottle of the beer and poured myself a glass of lemonade and brought them back to the living room. I handed Travis the bottle, our hands touching for a moment, and his fingers lingered on mine before he pulled the bottle back.

"Thanks," he said as he took a sip and sat back down.

I took a sip of my lemonade and held it in my hand. I knew at some point the conversation was going to veer towards us, I just wasn't sure when that would happen.

Travis put his beer on the coffee table on a coaster there and looked at me.

"Why did you leave me, Sophie?" he asked with a pained look on his face.

"Oh, Travis," I said to him. I could feel a knot forming in my stomach again. "When you told me what you wanted, that you were leaving school and what you wanted to do, part of me was excited about the possibilities, but another part of me was too scared. I didn't know what my life would be like without school, in a new place, far away from home. I was worried about it, and what would happen if you got to a bigger area and decided I was too "small town" for you anymore. Where would that leave me? I wasn't ready for that. Then when I talked about it with my mother, she was completely against it. She told me that wasn't part of the plan and I needed to focus on me. I was too confused, too hurt by the thought that you wanted me to give up all I knew. And I was too afraid to do it. I thought the safest thing was just for me to leave, go back to school and give you the chance to forget about me. It was the hardest thing I have ever had to do in my life."

"You could have come with me," Travis said, rising up from the couch. "I would never have abandoned you like you thought I would. You were my world, Sophie. You meant more to me than anything else. And you just tossed me aside without even a goodbye. That was hard to live with."

Travis walked over and looked out the front window onto the quiet street. I walked up behind him, feeling a mixture of sadness, but also some anger myself.

"You could have come after me too you know," I said to him with a raised voice. "You never once even tried to contact me after that. Not at school, not here, not anywhere. All this time Travis, I have been right here in our hometown, and you never once came looking. What was I supposed to think? In my mind, you were gone."

Travis turned to look at me know, and I could see some of his own anger on his face.

"Me? What about you?" He said with a raised voice. "You've been living in the same town with my mother for the last eight years. You know her, know where she is, and you never asked about me either, about where I was or what I was doing. Maybe if I knew…" His voice trailed off.

"If you knew what Travis?" I nearly yelled.

He stepped right up in front of me and gripped my upper arms in his hands.

"If I knew you were here, I would have come back sooner," he whispered. " I would have come back to do this." In a flash, he bent down and gave me a deep kiss. I could feel myself melting into his arms as I resisted just for a second before I threw my arms around his neck and kissed him back.

The kiss was long, slow and sensual, When we slowly broke from the kiss, my eyes were barely open, looking up into his eyes.

"I never stopped thinking about you Sophie," he said to me. "Not for one day. I always figured you met someone else at school, someone perfect for you, and you just moved on. That's why I never came back to Canon. I couldn't bear the thought of hearing about you being happy with someone else."

I embraced Travis tightly, holding myself against him. I could feel my eyes welling with tears.

"That's why I never asked your mother about you," I said, choking back the tears. "I didn't want to know that you were doing well, with someone else. The thought broke my heart. There's never been anyone else, Travis. It's always been you."

Travis broke our embrace and kissed me again, even more passionately than the first one. He put his hands around my waist as he kissed me over and over, and I never wanted that to end. We slowly walked each other over to the couch, where we sat down next to each other and kept kissing. I could feel my body getting warmer with each touch and embrace. Every time his lips touched mine I felt like it was taking my breath away. Travis began to kiss my neck, and I could feel the light stubble on his face rubbing against the nape of my neck. I felt myself lowering myself down onto the couch, so I was laying down, with Travis practically on top of me. My body was pressed against his as he kept kissing my lips, cheeks, and neck. I could also tell that he was clearly aroused himself at this point.

"Travis," I whispered breathlessly as he kissed me again, "let's.. let's go upstairs."

Travis looked up at me and nodded and got up from the couch. He took my hand and helped me up, and I led him up the stairs to my bedroom. I flipped the light on as the sun was practically set now and the dusk could barely light the room on its own. I stood in front of the bed, staring at him, and pulled him closer to me. I began to slowly unbutton his shirt, my hands trembling as I moved from button to button until they were undone. I pushed his shirt open and could feel the ripples of muscle on his chest. He shrugged out of his shirt, and I saw that he was in amazing shape. A smile crept across my face as I placed my hands on his chest and moved them down over his rock-hard stomach, feeling each muscle with my fingers.

Travis stepped back a bit and took off his boots, and then moved back toward me again. He bent down to kiss me once more, and as he did, my hands unconsciously went towards his belt buckle. I opened his belt and the button on his jeans and began to unzip them. I felt Travis' hands go to the back of my dress and unzip it easily. I heard and felt the zipper sliding down my back to the top of the skirt part of the dress.

We separated briefly from each other as I watched Travis tug his jeans down, leaving him in his tight black boxer briefs. I slid my dress off my left shoulder, then my right, and slowly shimmied the dress down my body until it fell at a pile at my feet, leaving me in my white bra and panties. I thought it would feel odd having a man look at me in this state of undress, but nothing felt weird about this moment.

"My God, Sophie," Travis said lightly to me. "You are so beautiful." Travis walked up to me and kissed me deeply again, letting his tongue mingle into my mouth. I kissed him back deeply, pressing my body as close as I could get to him.

Travis leaned forward and was on top of me on the bed. Our hands eagerly explored each other's body, I could feel his hardness pressing tightly against me now in his briefs. He moved his lips from mine, and they went down to the tops of my breasts, kissing each one lightly as he went along. I felt his left hand reach behind me and deftly unclasped the bra, and he gently pulled it over my shoulders until it was off my arms. He tossed it aside and hungrily went back to kissing each breast. Electricity shot through me as he took my left nipple into his mouth, kissing it and gently taking it between his teeth, while his right hand caressed my right breast. I could feel my body getting hotter and hotter with each thing he did to me, and I was grinding my hips against his to get more friction between us.

Travis' right hand slowly moved down from my breast, tracing the curve of my body until it was on my hip. He moved his hand, so it was just over the outside of my panties, and I am sure he felt the warmth and heat radiating from my body. He rubbed his hand lightly on the outside of my panties, making me moan in pleasure. I put my hand up into his brown hair and brought his lips back down to my breast. He kissed me and rubbed me at the same time, working me into a quick frenzy.

Before long, I could feel Travis tugging at my panties, slowly easing them down my legs. He pulled himself away from my body so he could finish taking my panties off me, leaving me completely naked. I looked at him and watched as he then pulled down his own briefs, letting his erection spring free. The sight of him took my breath away.

Travis began to come back over to me. Before he could do anything, I whispered out, "Travis... I'm... I'm still..."

Travis halted what he was doing and looked at me lovingly. He laid on the bed, just to my right, next to me, as his fingers traced up and down my body.

"Do you want me to stop?" He asked me gently.

I smiled over at him. "Oh God, no," I said, wanting him now more than I had ever in my life. "I just... I just thought you should know."

He leaned over and placed his right hand on my cheek, bringing my face to his so he could kiss me again. He slowly climbed back over my body, kissing me between my breasts. I could feel his erection just outside of me. I wasn't quite sure what to expect next. I wanted him, wanted him so badly, and my body was ready and waiting for him, but part of me was still nervous.

Travis slowly eased himself inside me, just barely at first. I gasped a little when I first felt him in me.

"Everything okay?" he asked me. He inched a little further into me as my gasp turned to a light moan.

"Hmmm Hmmm," I moaned out. The feeling inside me was incredible as he moved a little further inside, and then he began to develop a slow, rocking rhythm of thrusting that made my heart flutter. I didn't want the feeling to end, ever, and wrapped my legs around his waist, trying to pull him closer to me. Travis thrust deeper inside me, and we both groaned at the motion together. I peered up at him, with my eyes barely open, and I could see him looking down at me, watching how my body reacted to his so he could meet my needs. This sight turned me on even more than before, and my body seemed to open up even more to him.

We found a good rhythm together, rocking back and forth. I pulled Travis closer to me as I wanted to feel his body as close to me as possible. His chest was pressed hard against mine, he was kissing my neck, and I knew I was getting close. Travis kept up the rhythm until I let out a cry and gripped his body tightly, holding it against me as wave after wave of pleasure exploded in me. I then felt his orgasm deep in me as he groaned, and we held each other tight.

Travis kissed me deeply time and again and I felt like I would never catch my breath. He rolled off me to my right again, and this time took me in his arms to hold me close to him. We both lay there, panting and feeling the afterglow of our experience.

"How are you feeling?" Travis asked me as he caught his breath.

"Um... I don't feel like cooking dinner, that's for sure," I told him as I snuggled closer to him.

19

Travis

It was a pretty amazing night. I never imagined that what started out as a simple dinner would end up the way it did with Sophie, but I couldn't be happier that it worked out that way. We spent the whole night holding each other, touching each other, and exploring each other's bodies. Sophie was incredibly responsive to everything, and each moment seemed to bring out something new in her. Finally, at around three in the morning, we lay together on her bed amid the rumpled blankets, my right arm around her, cradling her head on my shoulder.

Sophie gently ran her hands over my shoulder, taking a look at the tattoo that was there of the rock with Abby's birthdate in the center.

"Why a rock?" she asked me gently as her fingers traced the tattoo.

I turned my head to look at her. "A couple of reasons," I told her. "First, obviously, it relates to our name."

"Ugh, how could I not have seen that?" Sophie said, feeling embarrassed she missed the connection.

"It's okay," I said, smiling at her. "Your brain isn't exactly concentrating on stuff like that at the moment."

She blushed at the statement. "So what else is it for?"

"Well," I explained, " I think it was because I have always seen Abby as my rock, the one thing in my life that has always held me together, kept me grounded. She's probably the strongest person I know, even if she doesn't see it all the time."

"That's sweet," Sophie answered as she nuzzled her head into the nape of my neck. "You should tell her that, Travis. She probably would love to hear it."

"I guess I could, though I don't know if she would listen to me right now."

"I think she pays attention to you more than you realize. I am sure she adores you. All girls feel that way about their dads."

I could see a little sadness on her face since she never got to have that kind of relationship with her father. I leaned over and kissed her.

"Shit," I said, sitting up quickly. "Is it really 3 AM? Abby and my mother are probably wondering where the hell I am." I stood up from the bed, looking for my pants that had my cell phone in it. Sophie rolled over onto her stomach and watched me run around the room naked trying to find my pants. As I picked them up, I could see her smiling mischievously at me.

"What's so funny?" I asked as I found my pants and grabbed my phone.

"You just look cute scampering naked in my bedroom," she said to me, as she rolled onto her back again, looking up at me upside down now, showing her own naked body to me. It made me want to toss my phone aside and get back to bed.

I glanced down at my phone. No messages from Abby or my mother, which seemed odd. I shot my mother a quick text to let her know I was still at Sophie's and to check on Abby. I got a reply back from her faster than I thought:

"I figured as much. Abby is sound asleep in my bed with me. She worked hard all night at the restaurant. We didn't get back until 1. Don't worry about her. All is well. Enjoy your night."

It was weird to get the okay from my mother to spend the night with a woman, but I was glad to read it.

"Everything okay?" Sophie asked me, rolling in the sheets now. I put my phone on her nightstand and climbed back up on the bed with her.

"Perfect," I said as I took Sophie in my arms again, pressing my body to hers. Feeling her body next to me like that, I could feel myself getting aroused again.

Sophie peered up at me. "My, my Mr. Stone, you do have an insatiable appetite."

I looked at her hungrily, feeling a burst of energy all of a sudden. I began to kiss my way down her body, going over every angle, placing gentle kisses between and on her breasts. As I kissed her stomach, I could feel her inhale in excitement, making her stomach taut. I kept going lower, with no intention of stopping, until I found myself kissing between her thighs. She slowly parted them to give me more room and invite me to keep going lower.

I found my lips exploring the soft blonde hair she had, brushing them against my lips. I could see the goosebumps forming on the inside of her thighs as I did this a few times to heighten the arousal even more. I could feel her feet turning in the sheets below me and took a quick glance up and could see that Sophie had closed her eyes and was breathing a bit harder. It was a good cue to me that I was going at the right pace for her.

I gently moved my lips downward, kissing her labia, which caused her to writhe a bit more. I nudged my lips a little deeper, moving them barely inside her, and let my tongue dart out slowly. Sophie let out a low moan, and I began to move my tongue around a bit more, exploring her, tasting her, feeling her dampness on my lips and tongue.

I loved tasting her, feeling her move with me, and watching her as she reacted to each motion of my face, lips, and tongue. I peered up at her again and could see that she was biting her lower lips, her eyes closed, and her fists clenched on the sheet beneath us. The tip of my tongue barely grazed her clit, and I could feel her hips arch on the bed. I used my hands to grasp her hips tightly as I kept licking and nibbling at her. I could feel her body starting to tremble as her breaths came faster and faster until she finally gasped loudly and stiffened her body. I could feel her share her orgasm with me as I kept kissing her deeply.

Sophie started to regain her composure as her body calmed down. I laid my head on her left thigh, watching her as she stretched and ran her fingertips over her ultra-sensitive body. She looked down at me smiling, with a rosy glow to her face.

"That was incredible," she shared with me, as I crawled back up to the pillows at the top of the bed.

"I'm glad you enjoyed it," I told her as I put my arm back around her and held her. I could feel her fingers tracing my body until they reached the scar on my leg. I looked over at her, and I could see her noticing just how long the scar was.

She took a closer look at it and then brought her head back up next to my shoulder.

"The scar," she said to me. "It looks like it was deep," she said as if she wasn't sure how to broach the subject.

"It was pretty deep," I said, trying to look at it while she touched. "I lost a lot of blood."

Sophie followed the trail of the scar from my thigh all the way down to the end of my calf and then back up again.

"Were you scared?" she asked.

I thought about it for a second. "I wasn't scared for me so much," I replied. "With the job, you learn that you can't be scared of what may or may not happen. Otherwise, you don't do your job well, and other people die. I was scared for the people still in the house and what was happening to them. And for Abby, if something happened to me."

"I don't know how you do it," Sophie said as she lifted her fingers off my leg and ran them over the stubble on my face.

"Well, I don't do it anymore," I said dejectedly. "The department is retiring me. It's too much of a risk I guess to have a fireman with a limp leading the way."

"I'm sorry, Travis," she said sincerely. "I know it's an important part of you. I guess I always knew that. That's part of the reason I couldn't go with you back then. I knew how much it meant to you, and I was too afraid, afraid that something would happen to you and you would be gone."

"Part of me always thought that was the reason," I said as I stroked her hair. I brought Sophie closer to me and held her tightly to me.

"You don't have to worry about that anymore," I whispered to her as I could feel her breathing soften as she fell asleep in my arms.

"I'm not going anywhere."

20

Travis

The morning sun shone through Sophie's bedroom early as the sun came up. I squinted from the gleaming light and glanced over at the clock on the nightstand. It was a little after 6 AM, and I had only had about two hours of sleep, but that didn't seem to matter much to me. I looked over and Sophie, still cradled in my arms. I tried to gently pull myself away, but as soon as I started to move, I saw her eyes flutter and start to open. She looked over at me, and I saw her smile radiate in the glow of the sun.

"Good morning," I said to her as I pulled my briefs on and grabbed my shirt.

"Good morning to you," she yawned, stretching under the thin blanket she had on. "Where are you going?" she asked me.

I tugged my jeans up and zipped them. "I know it's early, but it's Sunday. I thought maybe I could walk down to the bakery and grab some breakfast for us before they run out of everything." I sat on the bed to put my boots on.

"Oh, that sounds nice, but I want to come with you," Sophie said, standing up from the bed with the blanket still wrapped around her, partially covering her body. "Can you give me five minutes to throw something on?" she told me as she walked over to her dresser.

"Only if I get to watch you put it on," I said as I sat there on the bed, spying her every move.

She looked over shoulder at me and smiled, dropping the blanket to the floor so I could see her body from the back. I saw her deftly take a few items out of her top two drawers and then something out of a drawer to the left, watching her stretch so I could see her move and watch the outline and curve of her body. Sophie then turned to me and met my gaze as she dressed, stepping into the simple white cotton panties she had. I was entranced by every move, from her tugging the panties to her waist, to the shorts she stepped into shortly after, to the way she put her bra and t-shirt on. When she was done, she gave a curtsey to let me know the performance was over.

Sophie grabbed a hair ribbon off her vanity and tied her hair in a ponytail and stated she was ready to go. We walked down the stairs and out the door into the beautiful August morning. The air was crisper than it had been the last few days, and Sophie came close to me as she held my hand as we walked along the street. We reached the corner of Collins where my house was now, and we slowed down.

"Do you want to come in and look around?" I asked Sophie, as I pulled the keys from my jeans pocket.

"Sure, I guess so," she said as I opened the gate and let her walk through first.

"Be careful on the porch," I warned her. "The boards are not in great shape."

I stepped towards the front door to unlock it when I saw a look of terror on Sophie's face.

"What's wrong?" I said to her.

"Travis," she whispered as she stepped back. "I just saw something moving around inside, by the window."

"Wait here," I said to her as I quickly unlocked the door and swung it open to move inside. I saw a shadow move quickly as I entered and it moved towards the kitchen to go out the back. I knew I couldn't move that fast with my leg, but I went the opposite way down the hall and into the other entrance to the kitchen, hoping to cut whoever it was off. I saw them going out the back door as I entered the kitchen.

They moved quickly out the back door, and I heard a board crack as the hit the back porch. I made it out to the back to see a board splintered on the porch and the stranger laying on the ground with a skinned knee. They tried to scramble to their feet, but I swung myself off the porch and was able to grab a sleeve of the hooded sweatshirt they were wearing to hold them in place.

"Let go!" I heard a high voice yell.

I pulled the hood back on the shirt to reveal the face of a girl, smudged with a bit of dirt and with a small cut on her cheek. It was the girl from the picture I had found in Dad's car.

"Hold on, hold on," I told her trying to get her to calm down. She kept fighting to get away until I picked her up and brought her over my shoulders, carrying back towards the house.

"What are you doing?" she squealed.

"It's called a fireman's carry," I told her.

I carried her back inside, trying to avoid her kicking legs and her attempts to punch or scratch me. When I got into the living room, Sophie was in there to see me. I placed our trespasser on the couch. She immediately tried to get up and run, but I pushed her back down on the couch cushions.

"Stay put," I said to her. "You're hurt and need me to look at your leg, and you have some questions answer."

She struggled a little before sitting back on the couch, crossing her arms over her chest.

"Stephanie?" Sophie said, taking a closer look at the girl before sitting on the couch next to her.

"Yes, Ms. Ingram," she said resignedly.

"You know her?" I asked Sophie, looking over at her.

"She was a student in my class last year," Sophie said to me. "Stephanie Winters. Stephanie, what are you doing here?"

Stephanie looked at Sophie, then at me, and then back at Sophie, without answering.

"I can just leave it up to the police then," I said to her taking out my cell phone.

"Travis, wait, please," Sophie said.

"You're... you're Travis?" Stephanie said to me with a shaky voice.

"Yes," I told her. I think she was starting to put the pieces together just like I was.

"How do you know Travis?" Sophie asked her, wondering what was going on at this point.

"I think I can explain that Sophie," I said as I sat down in Dad's old armchair. I reached into my back jeans pocket and pulled out the picture of Dad with Stephanie and her mother. I handed the picture to Sophie, who took a look at it.

"It's your Dad," Sophie said to me, surprised to see Stephanie in the picture.

"And Stephanie's father too, right Stephanie?" I said, looking over at her. Stephanie took the picture from Sophie and looked at it, tears forming in her eyes. She just nodded at me as she sobbed.

"This… this is the picture I've been looking for," she said as she wiped the tears on the sleeve of her sweatshirt. "Where did you find it?"

"It was inside his truck in the garage," I said to her.

"I didn't have the key to the garage; I only had keys to the house. Well, they are Mom's keys, but I swiped them to come look for the picture." Stephanie looked over at the picture again and smiled, happy to have it in her hands.

"That means you two are brother and sister?" Sophie asked, still piecing everything together.

"Well, half-siblings I guess," I answered. "Let me see if there's anything in the medicine cabinet to clean up your knee," I said, slowly getting out of the chair.

"The first aid kit is under the sink in the kitchen," Stephanie told me.

I just nodded to her and went into the kitchen to get it. Sure enough, there was a first aid kit there. I walked back into the living room to see Stephanie and Sophie talking. I opened the kit to find some antiseptic to clean the wound and then used a small bandage and some tape to put over it.

"It's not bad," I told Stephanie as I finished putting the dressing on. "You'll be fine."

"Thanks," she said to me, slowly flexing her knee.

"So are you the one who cleaned up the house?" I asked her as I slowly got up from kneeling myself, feeling some soreness in my leg.

"Yes," she told us. "After... after Dad died, Mom didn't want to come to the house to get any of our stuff herself. She said it would be too painful for her, but she didn't want anyone else finding her stuff here. She and Dad always kept things pretty quiet. She.. she didn't want to upset your mother anymore," she said as she looked over at me.

"When I got here that first time, the house was pretty messy. Mom and I always cleaned up whenever we were here, but we hadn't been in here in about a week. It took me a few trips, but I got everything cleaned up and took our stuff, but I wanted this picture and couldn't find it. It was the only picture of the three of us. Dad never let us take a picture together, but we took this one at Fourth of July in the park."

I could see her hand trembling a bit as she held the picture. I never imagined that Dad's death would be hard for anyone, but clearly, I was wrong. He had created a different life for himself, and it looks like he was trying not to mess this one up.

"Does your mother know you have been coming here still?" I asked Stephanie.

"No," she replied. "She never asked for the keys back, so I kept coming, looking for the picture, straightening up. I would come in the back door and come early in the morning or at night when I didn't think anyone would notice I was here."

"So it was you I saw here the other night," Sophie said to Stephanie. "I thought it was just my imagination."

"It was me," Stephanie confessed. "I thought I was caught for sure when I saw you look at me, Ms. Ingram," she said with a smile, sniffling her tears away.

The three of us sat there in silence for a little bit, wondering what to do next. I stood up from my seat and took Sophie's hand, pulling her up off the couch.

"Sophie and I were going down to the bakery for some breakfast," I said to Stephanie. "Do you want to come with us?"

Stephanie looked at the two of us, and a smile brightened on her face. "I could go for some breakfast," she said, getting up off the couch.

I opened the front door for the ladies to go through, Stephanie first, followed by Sophie. Sophie stopped to give me a kiss before she went out the door.

"What's that for?" I asked her, pleased that I got a kiss.

"Because you are a good man, Travis Stone," she said with a smile.

I followed the ladies out the door. Sophie and I walked down the street, hand in hand, while Stephanie walked to the right of me, with one foot hopping up and down off the sidewalk in the street. Like everything else in Canon, the bakery was close by, about two blocks before the Homestead. We walked in, and there was only one other person in there getting some donuts. Sophie and Stephanie sat at one of the small tables in the corner by the front window while I went up to order.

The bakery has been owned by the same family, the Castellis, for many years. I had actually gone to school with the son of the original owner, and I saw Michael heading into the back as a young girl came out to wait on me. I ordered three jelly donuts and a few blueberry turnovers. I also got coffee for myself and Sophie, and hot chocolate for Stephanie.

I got back to the table holding the donuts and turnovers in a bag and placed it on the table. The young girl from behind the counter than brought over the beverages, proudly balancing the mugs on a tray without spilling a drop.

Stephanie happily took the hot chocolate, making sure to swipe all the whipped cream off the top with her finger first. She devoured a jelly donut, and then another, and probably would have gone for a third if Sophie and I hadn't decided to split it ourselves.

"Are you ready for high school in a few weeks, Stephanie?" Sophie asked as she sipped her coffee.

"I guess so," Stephanie said, not looking thrilled about the prospect of school, let alone high school. "It should be fine, I just wish the girls weren't such bitches," she said, taking a long draw on her hot chocolate.

I nearly had coffee come out my nose when she said this as Sophie looked at me.

"Sorry for swearing, Ms. Ingram," she said.

"It's okay," Sophie told her, as she shot me a look as I was trying not laugh out loud.

When we had finished our breakfast, we walked out of the bakery and stood out front for a minute.

"Well, thanks for breakfast," Stephanie said to me. "Will I... get to see you again?" she questioned.

Sophie looked at me to see how I was going to answer. I smiled at her and then at Stephanie.

"I think I am going to be around for a while, so the odds are pretty good," I told her.

"Great!" Stephanie said. She surprised me by giving me a hug, wrapping her arms around my midsection tightly.

"Bye Travis, bye Ms. Ingram!" she waved as she headed off in the direction of Collins.

"Do you think she is going back to my house?" I asked Sophie.

"No, she is probably going home. She only lives a few streets from behind your place, over on Gentry Street," Sophie remarked.

We started walking down the street, and Sophie took my hand again.

"So where to now Mr. Stone?" she said to me playfully.

I smiled over at her as we walked on.

"Now I take you home to meet my family," I told her as we turned towards my Mom's house.

21

Sophie

I have to admit I felt a little nervous as we walked along the streets of Canon towards Maggie's house. I hadn't been inside the house since before I went back to school without Travis some fourteen years ago, but that wasn't what I was nervous about. I was nervous about Abby, what she would think, and if she was ready to share her father with somebody else.

Travis could see something on my face as we got closer and closer to the house. We stopped just short of the driveway of the house. It was still early, barely past 8:30 in the morning, so we both knew Maggie was still there, and it meant Abby was there too. On top of everything else, I was walking into the house with both of them knowing that Travis had just spent the night at my house.

"Everything okay?" Travis asked me as he took my hand and looked into my face again with concern.

"Yes," I said, squeezing his hand in mine. "I'm just a little nervous is all."

"Nervous about what?" Travis said as he gently tugged me toward the driveway. "You've known my mother for over twenty years. She'll be happy to see you."

"it's not that Travis," I said to him, taking a serious tone. "It's Abby. What if she isn't okay with you seeing me? She might not like the idea that you spent the night with me."

"That's nuts," Travis said to me. He could see his statement got to me.

"I'm sorry, Sophie, that came out wrong," he said, taking both of my hands in his now. "Look, I barely dated anyone over the last twelve years. It's just been Abby and me most of the time, and I get why you might think that way, but you have nothing to worry about. If anything, Abby was always trying to get me to go on dates. All I did was work and spend time with her. I think she'll be glad to have someone to take the spotlight off of her for a change." Travis smiled at me as he said this, trying to get a smile out of me. I had no choice but to crack.

"Okay," I told him, taking a deep breath. "Let's go. But you better be right," I warned him.

Travis and I walked up the driveway towards the front porch of the house. He quietly opened the front door, and we slipped inside. He was listening for any sounds of activity when he heard some stirring in the kitchen. He nodded to me, took my hand, and we walked down the hall to the kitchen to see Maggie there, percolator in hand, pouring her coffee. She was already dressed for her day at the restaurant.

"Well good morning," she said to both of us, smiling. "Can I get you two some coffee?" she asked as she held up the coffee pot.
"Thanks, Mom, that would be great," Travis said as he went to get a cup. "Sophie?" he asked me as he held up an empty mug.

"Please," I said quietly, feeling too nervous still. I looked around the room, and it seemed like I was back to where we were all those years ago.

"Sit down, Sophie," Maggie said to me with a gentle smile, pointing to the chairs at the table.

Travis brought the mugs to the table and took the coffee pot from Maggie, pouring us each a mug. Maggie sat down at the table across from me while Travis leaned up against the counter, sipping his coffee.

"Did you to have a nice dinner last night?" Maggie asked as she took a sip, peering over the edge of her mug at me. I could feel myself turning red from the question, and looked at Travis, who was smiling at me, knowing we never even got to eat dinner.

"It was great Mom," Travis interjected.

"Well we had quite a night at the restaurant," Maggie told us. "The place was wall to wall people all night long, and not having a regular bartender there really put a crimp on things. I was running ragged all night long."

"You're going to have to hire someone fast Mom," Travis said to Maggie. "You can't keep up like that every day."

"You're right Travis, I can't," Maggie said, motioning to him to sit down in the chair next to me. Travis sat down next to me, putting his arm around me as we sat. I could see Maggie smile broadly as he did this.

"I had a proposition, and I wanted to see what you thought about it," Maggie said to us. "Since you have the house in town now, there's no sense in it going empty. If you're planning on staying around here, I'd like you to come work with me. I'd make you a partner in the restaurant; you could run and manage the bar, and I'll take care of the rest. Then, when I retire, you and Abby can take the whole place. What do you think?"

I looked over at Travis, trying to hide how giddy the thought made me feel. It was the perfect answer for all of us – Maggie gets help in the restaurant and gets to keep it in the family, Travis gets a job, and I get Travis to stay in town. It sounded like a win-win-win for all of us.

I saw Travis rock back gently in the chair as he sipped his coffee, pondering the idea. He looked at Maggie intently as he did.

"Don't do that in my chairs, Travis," Maggie scolded. "You know how I hate that."

Travis rocked the chair forward, so all the legs came to rest on the floor. He put his coffee cup down on the table. He looked over at me, and I am sure he could clearly see the hope in my eyes.

"Are you sure you want to do that Mom?" he asked her. "That place has been your whole life."

"I know Travis," Maggie sighed. "But the long days and nights, every day, are starting to take a toll on me. I haven't had a day off in months, or a real vacation in years. With you there, I would know the place was in good hands, and I could start enjoying my life the way I should. Abby could work there while she went to school and maybe, someday, if she wanted, she could take over the place from you, and the place could stay in the family."

Travis looked over at me again, this time taking my right hand in his left hand.

"Are you sure you want me around here all the time?" he asked me.

I put my right hand gently on his cheek.

"I wouldn't want it any other way," I told him, with tears in my eyes.

"Well," Travis said, turning to Maggie, "I guess you have a bartender and a partner."

Maggie clapped her hands together in joy and came over and hugged both of us.

"What's all the hugging about?" a voice said from behind us.

All three of us turned to see Abby standing there in her t-shirt and shorts, still wiping her eyes as if she just woke up. Maggie stood up and went over to Abby, pulling her into the kitchen. I could see Abby looking at me as if she was wondering why I was there. I started to feel nervous again, and I am sure Travis could see it on my face as well. He took my hand again and held it in his.

Abby walked over and stood by the edge of the table. Travis pushed the bag of turnovers he got from the bakery down her way, and she anxiously opened up the bag and took one out. She bit off the corner of the frosted treat, still looking over at us.

"It looks like you and I are going to be sticking around for a while kiddo," Travis told her.

"We're going to live in our house?" she asked excitedly.

"Yes," Travis said to her. Abby raced over and threw her arms around Travis' neck, hugging him tightly.

"Oh Dad, thank you," she said happily, hugging him again. She practically pulled him right out of the chair she hugged so tightly. As she broke the hug, she took notice of how Travis was still holding my hand. Her eyes went from me to her father, and back again. Abby then reached over and took my other hand.

"Can I borrow Ms. Ingram for a few minutes?" she said to her father as she pulled me out of my chair. I got up and followed Abby down the hall and out the front door. She sat down on the front step, and I sat next to her. I was a little worried about what was coming next.

"You two were more than friends, weren't you?" Abby asked me pointedly.

"Yes," I said to her honestly. "Your father and I were very close, right until he left to become a fireman."

"Oh," she said looking down at her feet. "So you were with Dad before he met my mother?"

"I was," I answered.

"I don't remember her at all," Abby said. She looked over at me, and I could see she was feeling a little sad about it. "Dad has shown me a few pictures he has of her, but that's all I know. I know I look like her, but I don't know anything else about her. Other than Grandma, I've never really had any other women around. Dad never dates much, and when he did, I never met any of them anyway. It's nice to know he has someone that makes him happy like that in you. And if we're going to be around here, maybe... maybe you and I can get to know each other better?" she said as she looked at me.

I felt a little choked up by what she just said.

"Absolutely," I told her. I reached over and held her hand lightly, and she gave my hand a little squeeze as she smiled at me.

Travis came out the front door and saw us sitting there. He squeezed his way between the two of us, putting an arm around each of us.

"You girls doing okay?" he asked us, looking back and forth between us.

"Dad," Abby complained to him. "We're not girls; we're ladies, right Ms. Ingram?"

"You're right, Abby," I said to her as I looked over at her. "Travis, make sure to call us young ladies," I said to him with a smile.

"And Abby," I said, leaning over Travis towards her, " You can call me Sophie."

22

Travis

After everything that happened Sunday – meeting Stephanie Winters, bringing Sophie back to the house, accepting Mom's offer of a job and business, and Abby and Sophie hitting it off – I was glad to just relax for the rest of the day. After the four of us spent the better of the morning together, laughing and enjoying the nice weather outside, Mom announced she needed to leave to get to the restaurant and wanted to know who was going with her.

"I guess I should go," I said to her, "so I can start getting used to things around here. Are you coming, Abby?" I asked as she and Sophie were whispering back and forth to each other on the porch.

"Heck yeah I'm coming," she said, feeling excited. "I've made good money in tips the last two days. I'll be able to get that new computer in no time," she said happily.

"Or, you can start putting money away in a bank account, like a responsible young lady," I added.

Her smile disappeared as I said it. "Really?" she asked me.

"Really," I told her. "We'll work on it."

Sophie got up from sitting on the porch and dusted her shorts off.

"I should get back home and let you three get to work," she said with a smile. I walked over and took her hand and walked her to the end of the driveway.

"Will I get to see you later?" she asked me, looking into my eyes.

"We'll probably get done around eleven or so," I told her. "Can I come by to see you that late, or will the neighbors talk about you?" I said with a grin.

She stood on her tiptoes and whispered in my ear. "Let them talk," she said, grinning back an even bigger smile. I kissed her gently, holding the kiss for a bit as I pulled her close by her waist. When we broke the kiss, she seemed a little out of breath.

"Oh my, Mr. Stone," she said wryly. "You took my breath away."

Sophie separated from me and started to walk down the street back toward her home.

"You do the same to me, Ms. Ingram," I shouted after her. Sophie turned to me and smiled as I watched her walk away. I turned back to face the house and saw Mom and Abby there, standing there watching me. They were both smiling at me as if they were trying to hold in laughter.

"What's so funny?" I asked as I walked toward them both.

"Nothing at all Travis," Mom said to me as she nudged Abby with her elbow.

"Nope, nothing," Abby added. "Except I never knew you were such a big marshmallow," she said, and she and my mother burst out laughing.

"What are you talking about?" I said in my defense. " I was saying goodbye to her."

"It didn't look like a lot of talking," Abby said with a giggle.

"Alright, enough already," I said, shooing her inside. " Let's go get changed for work."

I went upstairs and took a quick shower, washing off the last day's activities, and decided I had better shave since I wanted to look decent if I was going to be working at the restaurant regularly.

I guess I'll have to figure out a way to get our stuff from Ridgefield to here, I thought to myself as I finished shaving off the last of the growth on my face.

I went down to my room to change, putting on another pair of jeans and the last decent-looking shirt I had packed with me, and got myself downstairs, where Abby and Mom were waiting for me. Abby was already dressed in a white shirt and black slacks, the outfit for the restaurant.

"You're wearing that to work?" Abby commented, looking me up and down.

"It's all I have with me," I answered, realizing I didn't have to explain myself to my twelve-year-old.

"Grandma got me work clothes; I am sure she can get some for you," Abby said with a laugh.

"I can get some stuff for you if you like Travis," Mom said as we walked out the door.

"Thanks," I said feeling embarrassed now. "At least until I can make arrangements to get our stuff moved from Ridgefield to here."

We walked the quick walk to the Homestead easily, and by the time we arrived, most of the staff for the day was already there, waiting for Mom to unlock the place. She let everyone in, calling a quick staff meeting first to let them know about the changes she had planned, how I was coming on as a partner and taking over the bar, and that some responsibilities would be shifted around. Everyone seemed to be okay with the move, and then we all set to work.

I tried to familiarize myself a bit more with the bar and where everything was, and when Mom wasn't doing her regular routines, she sat with me to talk about bar deliveries, invoices and showed me where everything was on the computer in the office. It was going to take some time for me to get used to everything, but thankfully Mom seemed willing to have a learning curve so I could get my feet wet and understand the business gradually.

As the day wore on and business picked up, I saw Irv Rogers come in and walk over to the bar. He sat himself down on a stool, barely, and ordered a beer.

"How are you Mr. Rogers," I asked as I brought his beer down to him.

"Call me Irv, please," he said as he wiped his sweaty brow with his handkerchief and took a long draw of his beer.

"Okay, Irv," I said to him. "Call me Travis."

"Thanks, Travis," he said as he took another sip. "Actually your mother had called me asked to stop by with some papers. Something about putting the business in a partnership. I just wanted to come down and go over the particulars with both of you."

Wow, she didn't waste any time, I thought.

Before I went to go get Mom, I paused a minute with Irv Rogers.

"Irv, I'm glad you're here. I wanted to talk to you about my father's paperwork." I watched him empty his mug of beer and hand the empty mug to me. I walked over to pour him another.

"Oh, everything is done on my end," he told me. "I sent death certificates to the appropriate parties, and the house and the bank account is in your name now. I filed everything with the insurance company too, so you should see that in the bank account shortly, maybe even as soon as tomorrow."

"Great," I said to him as I set my mind working as to what to do with almost $300,000.

Mom then joined us at the bar as we talked about setting up the partnership, and Irv had some paperwork we needed to sign and send he would draw up the rest of the papers tomorrow and have them for us as soon as possible. He polished off his second beer, shook our hands, and waddled out the door and into the dusk.

The rest of the day and night was pretty uneventful. The place wasn't nearly as busy as Friday or what I assumed Saturday was like, and by 10 PM the place had pretty much cleared out, and Mom called the last call. When all the patrons were gone, I worked at getting all the glassware in the dishwashers, straightened up and cleaned the bar, and helped everyone put the chairs up to clear the floor. Everything was done a bit after eleven, and Mom, Abby and I walked out the door. We slowly moved along the very quiet street, with Abby looking pretty tired.

"The hard work is taking a lot of you, huh?" I asked her.

"It is, but I like it," she said to me. "It's nice to have some friends… and money in my pocket," she told me. I put my arm around her as we walked and reached the Mom's house.

I took a step back as Mom and Abby walked down the driveway.

"I think I am going over to Sophie's," I said casually.

Mom and Abby smiled at me. Abby made smooching noises at me.

"Go to bed," I said to her in mock anger.

"I'm going," she yelled as she hustled down the driveway, singing "Dad and Sophie sitting in a tree, K-I-S-S-I-N-G…" before she got inside.

"Have a good night, Travis," Mom said to me. I walked back down the driveway and tapped her on the shoulder, so she turned to face me. I gave her a hug, holding her tight.

"Thanks, Mom," I said to her. "I know I haven't said it to you enough over the years, but thanks for everything."

We broke the hug, and I could see her eyes were cloudy.

"You're welcome," she said to me. "And thank you, for bringing you and Abby… and Sophie… closer to my life. Don't let her get away from you again," she said to me with a smirk.

"I don't intend to," I said to Mom. "I'll see you in the morning."

I watched Mom walk down the driveway and into the house, and then I headed over to Sophie's. I walked past my house, smiling at it as I went by, and imagined what life was going to be like living there, this close to Mom and to Sophie. I had everything I could want in life.

I walked up to Sophie's door at about 11:30, not knowing if she would still be awake. I lightly tapped on the screen door and peered inside.

"Come on in, Travis," I heard Sophie say from the living room. I walked in and saw her sitting in her rocking chair, reading a book. She put the book down and stood up, walking over to me. She was just wearing an oversized shirt as she came over and kissed me. We walked over to the couch and sat together.

"How was the restaurant tonight?" she asked me.

"Tiring," I told her. "It's going to take me a while to get used to everything, but I think it will be fine. But after not doing any work for a couple of months, it's taking a lot out of me."

"Maybe you should just go to bed," Sophie said to me, as she knelt next to me, kissing my neck. I looked over, and she smiled at me.

"That sounds like a great idea," I said to her. I got up from the couch and tripped a little as I went passed the rocking chair.

"Travis, are you okay?" Sophie said as she sprung up off the couch.

"I'm fine, I just tripped," I told her as I looked to see what I tripped on. I looked down and saw the brown backpack. I picked it up and held it in my hands, looking at it in wonder.

"You still have it," I whispered, looking at the worn gold initials on the bag.

Sophie came over and took the bag from me. "I use it every day," she told me. "I never stopped carrying it with me, from the day you bought it for me at the school bookstore. It's always been special to me, and lets me think of you."

I turned to her and kissed her deeply, holding her tightly as I did. I could feel the curves of her body under her shirt as I held her. I swiftly bent down and lifted her up, taking her in my arms, and carried her up the stairs, She gasped when I picked her up so easily, and then giggled the whole time as we went up the steps.

I placed her down on the bed and kissed her again, I hovered over her body, my arms on either side of her, as I leaned into her and kissed her some more. Before I knew it, she had put her hands on my sides and rolled me over, so that she was on top of me. Her hands quickly were unbuttoning my shirt, and she pulled it off me. She then went right to my belt and jeans, getting those off me as quickly as possible as well, making sure to get my boots off along the way. Sophie leaned back on top of me, now that I was just dressed in my black boxer briefs. I scooted myself back further onto the bed as she knelt between my legs. I felt her fingers running over my growing erection in my briefs as she felt everything.

Sophie hooked her fingers into the waistband of my briefs and stripped them down my legs. She stood twirling them on her finger before she tossed them across the room with a laugh.

"What are you doing?" I said to her, watching her in amazement.

"I just wanted to try a few things," she said mischievously. She was back on the bed with me, kneeling between my legs. I felt her index finger glide from the base of my shaft right up to the tip. Edging her fingertip around the tip. I tried watching her, but the feeling was so good I soon found myself putting my head back on the bed. She swirled her finger around and around, exciting me with each touch before she took me in her hand and with a slow, deliberate motion, stroked up and down. The feeling was amazing, and I wasn't sure how long I could hold out.

"Sophie," I whispered.

"Did you want something, Travis?" she asked me coyly as she kept stroking.

"Yes," I growled. " I want you."

"Hmmm," she purred. " I guessed that much."

She released her grip on me and slowly, tease me, lifted her shirt over her head, revealing her body beneath it. I felt her inch closer to me, and she was then lowering herself on top of me, enveloping me deep inside her. She was just as worked up as I was right away and moaned lightly as I slipped inside her. She began rocking her hips gently back and forth on me as she guided my hands up to her breasts. I caressed and kneaded her breasts in my hands as I moved in rhythm with her. Sophie steadily increased the pace, and I tried to match her, doing my best to hold on without completely losing it too soon.

I felt her grinding deeper on me until she was hitting just the right spot for both of us. My hands moved down from her breasts to her hips as I held on to her. Sophie was running her hands up and down my body, over my chest and down my stomach, over and over again as I held on to her. I could feel myself sliding easily and deeply in her now, and I couldn't take anymore. My body began to tense as I had her hips tightly as I groaned. I thrust up, causing her to gasp, as I had my intense orgasm. I was throbbing in her when I felt her tighten on me moments later as her orgasm washed over her and me.

Sophie collapsed against my chest, holding me inside her as she kissed my neck. We were both covered in a quick sweat, and her slick body rolled off me to my right. I held her close to me as we both caught our breath.

"Well that was a nice surprise," I rasped.

"I'm glad you enjoyed it," Sophie said in between heavy breaths. "I know I sure did. I've been thinking about doing that to you all day."

"I can't think of a better way to end the day," I told her.

We both worked our way up to the pillows at the top of the bed. Sophie lay on my shoulder as I held her close to me. She seemed to drift off to sleep quickly, with a cute smile on her lips as she sighed.

Life can't get much better, I thought as I closed my eyes and held her tightly against me.

23

Sophie

It was probably the best night of sleep I had in a very long time. I woke up still laying on Travis' shoulder. He was softly snoring. Obviously worn out from the last few days as well. Last night was an incredible experience for me, and I loved exploring this new side of me that Travis had opened up. Somewhere lurking beneath all those buttoned-up dresses were these pent-up feelings of sexuality, and now that I had the right man to explore them with, I didn't want them to be stopped. I couldn't believe I had waited around for Travis to come to my house just wearing that old, oversized t-shirt with no underwear at all, but something inside me said I wanted to take him last night, to see what that would be like, and I was not going to be stopped. I'm just glad he was so receptive to it. He had made the last few days full of love, wonder, and intense feelings for me, and I just wanted to find a way to do the same.

I slid out of bed and jumped into the shower quietly, washing up for the day. After I got out of the shower, I wiped my hand and the fogged mirror and saw my reflection. Even my face after a simple shower seemed like it was smiling and happier than it had been in a long time. I wrapped the towel around myself and went out into the bedroom and saw Travis still sleeping. I quietly picked out some clothes from my dresser and slowly started getting dressed. As I was clasping my bra, I heard a sigh come from the bed. I turned to look and saw Travis watching me with a big smile on his face. I smiled back, held up the yellow panties I was about to put in, and turned away from him so he could watch me slowly slide them up my legs and over my backside, while I looked at him over my shoulder so I could see him watch me.

I threw myself onto the bed next to him and kissed him good morning.

"What's the plan today before work?" I asked him as I tilted my head in the palm of my left hand and ran my right hand through the hair on his chest.

"I actually do have a couple of errands to run if you want to come with me unless you have stuff to do," he said to me.

"Nothing that can't wait a day or two," I said to him. My right hand had moved from his chest down to his hip and was steadily moving inward from there. Travis smiled over at me.

"I think I created a monster," Travis said with a laugh as he felt my hand on him.

"You have no idea," I said seductively, teasing him gently with my fingers. Travis rolled to his side to face me and kissed me.

"I would love to take you up on this, believe me, but I have to take care of this stuff. Can I make it up to you later?" Travis said to me as he kissed my neck.

"I guess so," I pouted. "But you will have to work extra hard," I told him.

"Oh I will," he promised.

Travis dressed quickly in the clothing he wore to the house last night. We walked casually over to Maggie's house, where Maggie and Abby were up and having breakfast.

"Morning Dad," Abby smiled. "Good morning, Sophie," she said to me just as happily.

Travis and I sat at the table, and I had some coffee while Abby got up and made us all eggs and bacon. Travis was astounded at what she was able to do.

"How come you never cooked like this at home?" he asked her.

"You never asked me to," Abby told him. "Besides, Henry showed me a few things when I was working in the kitchen the last few days. I've got mad culinary skills," she said as she twirled the spatula in her hand like it was a six-shooter.

"You may have another cook someday Mom," Travis said as he put another forkful of eggs in his mouth.

"You mean we will have a chef," Maggie corrected him.

"You're right. It's going to take some getting used to," Travis told her. He turned to look at Abby. "Abs, Sophie and I are running some errands this morning. Why don't you come with us and give Grandma a break?"

"Okay," she said. "Just let me go get dressed first." Abby put the dirty frying pan in the sink and headed off to go get dressed.

"I don't know who this friendly, agreeable kid is, but if you two bring that out in her I am all for it," Travis said as he put a piece of bacon into his mouth.

"She can stay with me if you two want some time together, Travis," Maggie said to him as she washed the frying pan.

"It's okay Mom" Travis answered. "I want her to come anyway. You can have some time to do things you need to do."

"Okay," she answered. "I do have some things to pick up at the dry cleaners this morning anyway."

"Didn't you just pick stuff up there Saturday?" Travis asked. I saw the look on Maggie's face like she was caught, and I quickly put two and two together.

"It's a restaurant, Travis," I cut in. "I'm sure there's stuff at the dry cleaners all the time, right Maggie?" I looked over at her, hoping she knew where I was going.

"Absolutely," she replied. "Uniforms, tablecloths, you name it. We're probably the main reason Fred Perkins is still in business."

"Funny you should mention him," Travis said to Maggie. "I ran into him at the florist when I was picking up flowers for Sophie on Saturday. The florist says he's been picking up the same bouquet there for years. I guess he's got a sweetheart too," Travis said as he finished the last piece of bacon and gave me a kiss.

Maggie gave me a sly smile as I kissed Travis back.

Way to go, Maggie, I thought to myself. I pulled Travis out of his chair as I heard Abby coming down the steps. "Let's go, Travis," I said to him. "We'll see you later, Maggie," I turned to look at her as we walked down the hall and I could see her mouth "Thank you" to me.

We met Abby at the door and climbed into Travis' car, a beat-up old Ford that looked past its prime.

As Travis pulled out of the driveway, Abby remarked from the back seat, "Hey Dad, why don't you drive that truck at the house instead of this old heap?"

"Hey," Travis said, sounding genuinely offended, "This old heap has served us well for a long time. That is a nice truck in the garage though. I just have to have the paperwork fixed on it."

We drove just a few short blocks over to Warfield Bank, the local bank in town. Travis parked in the lot and hopped out quickly.

"You two wait here," he said to us through the open driver's side window. "I'll just be a minute." He dashed off inside the bank before I could say anything else to him.

"What's he doing at the bank?" Abby asked me.

"I guess it's something to do with your grandfather," I told her, though I wasn't really sure what he was doing in there. We sat quietly for a minute or two before Abby piped up again.

"Sophie?" she said to me.

"Yes?"

"Do you think you and Dad are going to get married?"

I coughed a little and turned to look at her. Abby was smiling, waiting for an answer.

"I think we're a long way from making that decision just yet, Abby," I said to her. "We've only been together again for a few days."

"Oh, I know," she answered. "But he clearly loves you, and you love him, right?"

My heart skipped a beat. It was nice to hear Abby say that her father clearly loved me.

"I do love him," I said to her. "Don't worry, Abby. If he asks me one day, you'll be the first to know, okay?"

"Okay, great," she said.

Travis came walking back to the car thankfully, and climbed in, holding an envelope.

"What were you two gir... I mean young ladies talking about?" Travis asked as he started the car.

"Not much," Abby said to him. "Just marriage."

Travis nearly got hit by a car coming down the road as he was pulling out into the street and not paying attention to the road. He slammed on the brakes as the car went past, with the driver giving us all a nasty glare.

Travis waved to the driver, signaling a sheepish apology, as he pulled out on the road.

"What do you mean you were talking about marriage?" Travis asked, looking over at me.

"Don't look at me," I said defensively. "Abby brought it up."

"I just asked Dad; don't go crazy," Abby said as she looked at her phone casually. "I just told Sophie that since you love her, it might be nice if you got married one day is all. You do love her, right Dad?"

I looked over at Travis, and he was looking at me, not knowing what to say.

"Travis, you don't have to say anything…" I was saying until he interrupted me.

"It's okay," Travis said as he drove. "She's right; I do love you, Sophie."

I could feel tears in my eyes as he reached over and held my hand as he drove.

"I love you too," I said to him quietly.

We drove along for a bit, passing their house on Collins and then making a right. Travis drove up two blocks and then was making a right on Gentry.

"Travis, where are you going?" I said to him quietly, knowing what he was looking for.

"Which house is it, Sophie?" he asked me and pointed to the blue ranch house two houses down the street on the left. The plain silver mailbox had the name "Winters" on it, and Travis pulled into the driveway and turned off the car.

"What are we doing here?" Abby asked from the back seat.

"I have someone to talk to here, and there's someone I want you to meet," Travis said as he got out of the car. Abby and I each got out of the car as well and we walked up the short stone walkway to the front door. Travis knocked on the door, tapping his foot nervously as we waited for someone to answer. Moments later, the door opened, and Stephanie was standing there, with a shocked look on her face.

"Travis, Ms. Ingram... what are you doing here?" Stephanie said nervously.

"Hi Stephanie," Travis said to her through the screen door. "Is your mother here? I just... just wanted to talk to both of you for a minute."

Stephanie stood frozen for a minute before she opened the door. "She's in the kitchen having coffee before she leaves for work."

Abby and I trailed behind Travis as we walked in. Stephanie and Abby exchanged glances at each other, each wondering who the other was.

Travis strode into the kitchen with us behind him, and Stephanie quickly walked into the room. Emily Winters was seated at her kitchen table and looked up, shocked to see three guests in her home. She looked just like her picture and as I remembered her from parent-teacher meetings like she was just a slightly older version of Stephanie.

"Ms. Winters," Travis stated, "I'm..."

Emily cut him off. "I know who you are, Travis," she said as she stood up, looking like she was feeling a bit defensive for the moment. "Why are you here?" she asked him.

"I... was just hoping to talk to you for a few minutes," he said, trying to sound sincere. "I don't want to keep you if you're going to be late for work or anything, but I didn't think you would want to meet at the restaurant."

Emily sat back down in the chair and motioned for all of us to sit at the table.

"No, I haven't been to the Homestead since… well since that night," she said, her voice trailing off.

"I don't really have any right to take up your time. Your relationship with my father was your business. It's obvious to me, from what I have learned over the last few days," Travis took a look at Stephanie, "that you and Stephanie were very important to him. You were probably the most important things he had in his entire life. "

I could see Emily was starting to tear up. Stephanie walked behind her and put her hand on her mother's shoulder as Emily sobbed gently.

"He was a good man, you know," Emily said to us through her tears. "I know you may not have seen it Travis, but he always treated me well. After I got pregnant with Stephanie, I didn't know what would happen, but he was thrilled at the chance to be a father again. He took good care of me, and Stephanie."

"If you don't mind me asking," Travis said to her, "Why didn't he ever marry you? He clearly wanted you as part of his life."

Emily sighed. "He asked me to marry him several times before Stephanie was born and after. I always said no. I didn't want people talking, saying he only married me because he got me pregnant. People in Canon never thought much of him and always gave him a hard time. It would have been worse for all three of us if I had married him and we all lived together in that house as a family. I didn't want to be seen as worse of a homewrecker than I already was. I tried to get him to leave Canon, telling him I would marry him if we went somewhere else and started over, but he wouldn't. He said he had to prove to… to you, Travis… that he could take care of the house and leave something for you one day. So that's how we lived. I got a job over in Sterling as an office manager at my brother's contracting business, bought this house and fixed it up before Stephanie was born, and we've been here ever since. We would go over and see your father at night or on weekends, or we would meet out at the park or other places away from everyone else so we could be together. He was actually doing well and had cut back on drinking and everything. He was a different man than you knew, Travis. The heart attack caught us completely off guard. I... I didn't even go to the funeral."

Emily was openly crying now, and Stephanie held her mother tightly. Abby and I both had tears in our eyes as well. Travis stayed strong, but I could tell he was moved.

"I'm sorry... for everything Emily," Travis said to her. "You deserved to be happy, deserved to be recognized as his family more than I did." Travis took the envelope he had and slid it across the table to Emily.

"What's this?" she said as she picked up the envelope and opened it.

"It's a bank check for $275,000. That's what there was in Dad's life insurance policy and his bank account. You and Stephanie should have it."

Everyone at the table was staring with their mouths open. Emily opened the envelope and looked at the check.

"Travis," she said, wiping the tears from her eyes, "I can't take this from you. He left this to you for a reason." Emily tried to hand the envelope back to Travis, but he wouldn't take it.

"He left it to me for the wrong reason," Travis said to her. "He left it to me because he felt guilty about how he was with me and my mother. It belongs to the people he was closest to, and that was you two. He left me the house, which was more than he needed to, but that house is all I need for my family." He reached over and took my hand and Abby's hand and held them together. "Please, Emily take it. Use it for Stephanie's college, take a trip, do whatever you want, whatever you think he would have wanted you to do."

Travis pushed the envelope back to Emily, and she slowly picked it up, tears flowing from her eyes again.

"I don't know what to say," Emily said, sniffling through the tears. Stephanie came over to Travis and gave him a big hug.

"Thank you, Travis," she whispered into his ear.

Travis and Stephanie broke their hug. He turned and looked at Abby, who was stunned by all this.

"Abby," he said to her, "This is Stephanie. She's my sister." Stephanie gave Abby a shy wave, and Abby didn't know what to say.

"Wait a minute," Abby said, interrupting the moment. "If she's your sister, does that mean she's my aunt?"

We all looked at each other and realized it was true, making us laugh through the tears.

"It's okay," Stephanie said to Abby. "You can just call me Steph instead of Aunt Stephanie," she said with a smile.

Abby laughed out loud at this as well. Travis stood up from the table and Emily came over and hugged him, and then give me a hug as well, and then gave one to Abby for good measure.

"Okay, we don't want to keep you any longer," Travis said as he readied to go. We started walking towards the door as Emily and Stephanie followed us out. Travis got into the driver's side of the car, and Stephanie walked over to that side of the car.

"Would it be okay if I stopped by to see you at the house?" Stephanie asked.

"Any time you want," Travis told her, giving her a kiss on the cheek.

We backed out of the driveway and turned to head back towards Collins where the house was.

"Wow," Abby said. "That was pretty wild. You know what Dad?"

"What's that honey?" Travis said as he drove.

"You're a pretty awesome guy," she said proudly.

I saw Travis smile. "Thanks, Abby," he said sitting taller in his seat.

"You *are* an awesome guy," I said to him, holding his hand as we turned on Collins to go past the house and head towards the center of town.

24

Travis

Several days had passed since I drove over to give Emily Dad's money. I felt better that they have it, and I was sure they would make good use of it. In that time, I had gotten Dad's car straightened out with the DMV, so it was now in my name, making it okay for Abby to be seen with me while driving. Danny had started work on the exterior of the house, and the place already looked much better, with new gutters and new windows done, and Danny's crew working to fix the porches. I had gone back to Ridgefield to turn in my retirement papers at the department, and to give my landlord notice that we were leaving. I hired a local mover to clean the apartment out as fast as they could and get our stuff up to the new house so that everything was already arriving today.

Abby was all excited about the prospect of starting over in a new town. She and Stephanie had hung out a couple of times, getting to know each other, and I was glad to see she had made a new friend around her own age instead of just hanging out with the waitresses at the restaurant. Sophie had helped to get Abby enrolled in school, getting her paperwork together from her old school and setting her up with a schedule, though both Sophie and Abby were nervous that Abby would be in her English class.

I was doing my best to get settled in at the restaurant as well, giving my new career my all. I picked up on the inventory and ordering pretty quickly, made contacts with vendors, got to know the staff, and even hired another part-time bartender to help us out, so I didn't have to work seven days a week. Mom seemed to be glad that some of the burden was off of her now, and she even took to showing up later at the restaurant a few times instead of getting in so early each day.

Life with Sophie couldn't get much better either. We spent as much time as we could together, making up for all the time we didn't have together and got to know each other better again. I would go over to her place after work every night while they were working on my house and before it was furnished, and we would spend all night together talking, telling stories and getting to know each other physically and emotionally.

It had been a long, busy Friday night at the restaurant and I was glad to get out of there after cleaning up. Mom had even left a little earlier than I did tonight to give herself a break, and Abby walked over to Stephanie's house so they could have a sleepover there. I drove over to Sophie's and parked in her driveway. I walked up to the house and saw her sitting in her rocking chair, as usual, wearing a light blue cotton dress. I walked in and over to her and gave her a kiss as she went to stand up and took her by the hand and walked her out the door.

"Where are we going?" she asked me quizzically as we walked down the driveway and past my car.

"I thought we would take a little walk tonight," I said to her as I put my arm around her as we walked.

The late August night air was getting cooler, letting us know fall was not far away now. We walked a little ways up the block and crossed the street so that my house was only about a block away. Unusually, another couple was walking towards us, holding hands. As we got closer to the light of the street lamp, it became clear who it was. There was my mother, walking and holding hands with Fred Perkins.

Mom had a shocked look on her face when Sophie and I came upon them.

"Hi Mom, Mr. Perkins," I said with a sly smile.

"Oh Travis," Mr. Perkins said, feeling a bit befuddled. "Call me Fred, please."

"Where are you two off to?" I asked my mother.

"We're just out for a walk, enjoying the night air," she said to me. "You know how it's my favorite time to enjoy life in Canon."

"Yes, and now I know why," I told her. Sophie tugged on my hand, silently telling me to be nice.

"Well, you two enjoy your evening," Sophie said, jumping in, and making me walk down the street.

"You too!" Fred said back to us, picking up my mother's hand again as they kept walking.

Sophie ushered me down the street.

"How long do you think that has been going on?" I asked Sophie, turning back to make sure Fred was being a gentleman.

"I am guessing a while," Sophie said. "Instead of worrying about them, why don't you tell me where we are going."

I turned my attention back to her just as we got to my house on the corner of Collins. I opened the new cyclone fence gate for Sophie as she walked through on the freshly-manicured lawn. She took a look around smiling at all the improvements, including the new front porch, complete with its own white porch swing.

We sat down on the porch swing and moved it gently. Sophie put her head on my shoulder and sighed as we relaxed together.

"So what do you think of this small town life, Mr. Stone?" Sophie asked me.

"I don't think there is any place I would rather be, Ms. Ingram," I said to her.

"No place at all?" she asked, lifting her head up to look at me.

"Well, maybe one place," I said to her.

With that, I stood up and swiftly lifted her up, cradling her in my arms, and carried her across the threshold, pushing the door open so we could head upstairs to my bedroom.

No one keeps the doors locked in Canon you know.

www.ingramcontent.com/pod-product-compliance
Lightning Source LLC
Chambersburg PA
CBHW020842260626
47169CB00003B/1092